"ARE YOU HERE BECAUSE YOU COULDN'T STAY AWAY?"

In a single movement he was standing beside her, wrapping her in his arms, bending his fair head to hers. Her lips opened like blossoms seeking the sun and, when he kissed her, all thoughts of court seemed to vanish.

They kissed again and again, clinging to each other hungrily. Jan could feel the heat of his body and the rapid, strong beat of his heart through his jacket. The way he held her so possessively in his powerful arms sent her blood singing through her veins. She felt as if she were on a roller coaster, dropping through the sky, dizzy with a desire that could not be denied. . . .

TRICIA GRAVES was born in the beautiful West Virginia hills. At eighteen, she left home to travel, but her heart has always remained in the mystical mountains of her childhood. She considers herself a liberated woman with a strong streak of old-fashioned romanticism. In addition to writing, which is her first love, she also enjoys reading, sailing, playing the organ, driving, and caring for her family, her five cats and dozens of plants.

Dear Reader:

The editors of Rapture Romance have only one thing to say—thank you! At a time when there are so many books to choose from, you have welcomed ours with open arms, trying new authors, coming back again and again, and writing to us of your enthusiasm. Frankly, we're thrilled!

In fact, the response has been so great that we now feel confident that you are ready for more stories which explore all the possibilities that exist when today's men and women fall in love. We are proud to announce that we will now be publishing six titles each month, because you've told us that four Rapture Romances simply aren't enough. Of course, we won't substitute quantity for quality! We will continue to select only the finest of sensual love stories, stories in which the passionate physical expression of love is the glorious culmination of the entire experience of falling in love.

And please keep writing to us! We love to hear from our readers, and we take your comments and opinions seriously. If you have a few minutes, we would appreciate your filling out the questionnaire at the back of this book, or feel free to write us at the address below. Some of our readers have asked how they can write to their favorite authors, and we applaud their thoughtfulness. Writers need to hear from their fans, and while we cannot give out addresses, we are more than happy to forward any mail.

Happy reading!

Robin Grunder
Rapture Romance
New American Library
1633 Broadway
New York, NY 10019

HEART ON TRIAL

by
Tricia Graves

RAPTURE ROMANCE

NEW AMERICAN LIBRARY

TIMES MIRROR

PUBLISHER'S NOTE

This novel is a work of fiction. Names, characters, places, and incidents either are the product of the author's imagination or are used fictitiously, and any resemblance to actual persons, living or dead, events, or locales is entirely coincidental.

Copyright © 1983 by Tricia Graves

SIGNET, SIGNET CLASSIC, MENTOR, PLUME, MERIDIAN AND NAL BOOKS
are published by The New American Library, Inc.,
1633 Broadway, New York, New York 10019

First Printing, November, 1983

1 2 3 4 5 6 7 8 9

PRINTED IN THE UNITED STATES OF AMERICA

For Pat Bennett, Attorney at Law,
a liberated woman and a romantic lady.

Chapter One

❦

Janelle ran at a steady pace, ignoring the pain in her tender calf. She had started jogging less than a year ago and she didn't consider herself to be a "serious" runner, but she had to admit that she was hooked on it. To her, the sport was a love affair with nature, with the good, solid earth beneath her feet and the cloudless blue autumn sky above her head.

She lifted her face to the sun and let the gentle morning breeze catch her long, brown hair. Her old gray running shoes stirred up dust on the dry track and she knew that her face would be streaked with grime by the time she finished her course around the lake. But she didn't care. After the long, scorching New York City summer, she was running again!

When she was halfway around the lake, another runner passed her, moving easily, fluidly on long, tanned legs. The man had the grace of a dancer, the perfection of movement of a well-oiled machine. His broad shoulders tapered to a slim waist and narrow hips. His arms moved gracefully at his sides, in rhythm with his easy strides.

For a moment, Jan was mesmerized as the man seemed to float past her. Then, for some reason that she could not define, his straight back and effortless stride irritated her into action. She took a deep, lung-filling breath and drew upon a reserve of strength to pick up her speed and lengthen her stride. She pumped her arms and lifted her long, slender legs higher. Within seconds, she was running alongside the man, keeping pace with him.

He didn't throw a single glance in her direction, and that, too, irritated Jan. She was used to being noticed and singled out for attention by men wherever she went, and although she often complained about too-casual flirtation, she didn't particularly like being ignored either.

She forced herself to run even faster, to pull ahead of the tall, impressive man. She had started to perspire and was thankful that she had worn a sweatband to contain her cascading dark-brown hair and keep the perspiration out of her eyes.

The man began to pull away from her again, and stealing a glance at his face, Jan thought she saw the beginning of a smile on his lips.

She pressed herself to run faster, and although it took a little longer this time, she caught up with him and ran along beside him. The pain in her calf was becoming increasingly difficult to ignore, her body was covered with perspiration, and she was short of breath and aching with fatigue. But it was worth it. She was keeping up with her competitor and she felt as though she was winning a marathon. The exhilaration she felt was almost a sexual excitement, a tingling expectation that the best was yet to come. She didn't know how much farther her aching legs would carry her, but she was determined not to stop until he did.

When he finally let up a little on his pace and started to slow down, Jan wanted to say "thank you." Instead, she put on one last burst of speed and crossed the "finish line" a bare second or so ahead of him.

Then she fell to the grass beside the track, panting and breathless, her slim hands moving to the calf of her leg to massage the sore muscles.

A moment later, the man threw himself down beside her. He lay flat on his back, with one tanned arm flung over his face to shield his eyes from the sun, and Jan was pleased to see that he was as breathless as she was. Before he caught his breath to speak, Jan had a chance to look him over. He was tall, probably six or six-one, with long, muscular legs (a real runner!), broad shoulders, slim hips, and a flat stomach. His arms and shoulders were powerfully muscled and, even at rest, he exuded a hard, physical strength. His hair was longish, a warm sandy brown, and from the color of his skin, he looked as though he lived in the outdoors. His body emitted the scent of an expensive aftershave, which mingled with the raw odor of perspiration and something else Jan could only define as his "maleness."

All at once, she became aware that she was alone in the park with a complete stranger who was barely clothed in gray jogging shorts and a faded blue T-shirt that clung to him like a second skin. The shirt rippled over his well-muscled chest as he inhaled and exhaled slowly in an effort to control his erratic breathing.

Jan was starting to climb unsteadily to her feet when his deep voice stopped her cold.

"Do you always do things like that?" he asked.

"Like what?" she asked innocently, turning to face him. Her breath caught in her throat. He was watching her with the most beautiful, clear green eyes she had ever seen. She couldn't pull her eyes away from his; they were as cool and inviting as a deep pool in the depths of a dark forest. For a long moment, she was powerless to look away. Then her excitement turned to a feeling closely akin to fear as she realized that she could very easily become lost in those eyes.

"Like turning a nice morning run around the lake into a damned dead heat," he answered. He was smiling at her with those incredible eyes, although his full, sensuous lips were still and the tone of his deep-timbered voice was completely serious.

"I guess I should apologize for that," Jan answered lamely.

"You *guess?*"

"I don't know what came over me." She certainly wasn't going to tell him that the perfection of his body and the way he used it had irritated her into the competition.

"Well, whatever it was that came over you, I hope you take it with you to the marathon next month." His laughter came out full and strong, in sharp contrast to his carefully modulated speech.

"Oh, no!" Jan protested, rising to her feet with an easy grace that brought an admiring smile to the man's face. "You won't find me signing up for any marathon. I'm not really a serious runner."

"No?" He raised his eyebrows in mock surprise. "Well, you could have fooled me. Do you have a name, or should I just refer to you as my competitor?"

"Janelle. Janelle Richmond."

"Janelle . . ." She had never liked her name, the way most people pronounced it with two harsh syllables. Now, on this stranger's lips, her name was suddenly musical. He didn't just say it, he caressed it. She watched his full, sensuous lips form the word again. "Janelle. I don't think I've ever met a Janelle before."

She flushed and forced herself to look away from him. "Call me Jan—almost everyone does."

"Okay, Jan. I'm Blair Wynter." He was extending his hand, waiting for her to take it with an expectant smile playing on his lips.

"Glad to meet you, Blair." She smiled and casually took the strong, square hand that he offered. As soon as their hands touched, Jan's smile faded. A current of warmth overwhelmed her, followed by a tingling sensation that crept up her arm from their point of contact. She was suddenly quite self-conscious and she pulled her hand away a little too quickly.

He gave her a curious grin and a look that showed his own surprise. "Could I buy you a quick cup of coffee, Jan?" He glanced at the thin gold watch on his wrist.

"No, I can't. I have an—" She almost said "an early appointment with a new client," but she caught herself in time. Just the knowledge that she was a lawyer had dampened the enthusiasm of more than one attractive man. She had found out the hard way that most men didn't care to date aggressive, ambitious women. And this one was too gorgeous to turn off before she had had the chance to see him again.

"I have a date for breakfast," she lied.

"A date you can't get out of?" He was watching her with a strange half-smile on his lips and she wondered if he was making fun of her.

"Something like that," she answered, thinking of her nine-fifteen appointment with Carole Downing.

"I'm sorry. I would have loved to buy you breakfast myself."

"How about tomorrow morning?" she asked boldly.

"Are you buying?"

She nodded.

"How can I refuse? Just tell me where and when."

"Eight o'clock tomorrow morning, at Perroni's Restaurant."

"You're on," he answered. "Or, if you're running, we could meet at the park—" he started, but she cut him off.

"I'm not running tomorrow. I don't run every day. I told you."

"I know. You're not a serious runner. Okay, I'll meet you at the restaurant. Eight o'clock."

"See you tomorrow, then." Jan forced herself to turn and walk slowly through the park toward the exit road. She wanted to stop and look back, to make sure that he was really as handsome as she remembered him to be. But, somehow, she knew that he was still standing where she had left him, watching her retreat.

Well, tomorrow things will be different, she told herself. Tomorrow I'll have the upper hand and he'll be the one who has to retreat!

Satisfied with herself, Jan made quick work of exchanging her jogging outfit for a business suit and heading for work.

Her office was located on Broad Street in Lower Manhattan and she flagged a cab in front of her apartment building to take her there. During the ride downtown, she thought about her job and about what this morning's interview could eventually mean to her.

Jan had been with Babcock, Wynne & Whitmann for almost five years, since her graduation from law school. During that time, she had worked herself up from law clerk to associate, then to junior partner. Now she was ready for a change, ready to break away from the firm and set up her own office.

Jan had decided long ago that she would like to specialize in divorce and custody law, something she could not really do as long as she worked for Babcock, Wynne, where new cases were assigned to junior partners on a rather random basis. From Mark Whitmann's description of the case he had just given her to handle, it sounded as if this just might be the one she needed to launch her own office. There was nothing extraordinary about the case, but from all indications it was going to be a rather tough one and a good showing could do much to advance her career.

As the cab made its agonizingly slow way through the heavy morning traffic, Jan tried to concentrate on her day's schedule. It was going to be a busy day, but she loved her work and seldom got bored. However, even as she tried to keep a mental picture of her day's activities before her, her mind kept drifting back to the man in the park. Repeatedly she caught herself staring nowhere in particular with a secret smile on her lips as she remembered the wicked grin he had given her as she ran beside him, and the shocking warmth she had felt from the mere touch of his hand.

Jan dated several men casually, but no one was really special to her. She was becoming disillusioned with the old ideals she had once held, with the dreams that had once made her nights alone bearable. For some time now, she had doubted she would ever find the perfect man, the one who would make her want to marry him and have his children. But Blair Wynter was surely a fascinating man, and what would it hurt to dream the impossible dream just a little longer? Wasn't there a popular song a while back called "Please Be the One," or something like that? Well, maybe the mysterious Blair Wynter would be the one for her. He certainly had the face and the body for it, not to mention that deep, almost musical quality to his voice.

"Hey, lady, wake up!" The cabdriver was leaning over the seat, his wide, ugly face registering his disgust for daydreamers, even pretty ones.

Jan paid her fare, tipped the impatient man handsomely, and ran into the building, feeling that something momentous was about to happen, something that just might turn her life around completely.

A lone blond woman was sitting in the reception area nervously thumbing through a copy of *Vogue*.

"Is Mr. Whitmann in yet?" Jan asked Sue, the receptionist, thinking that it would be common courtesy to invite Mark to sit in on the first interview, if he was available.

"He's in court this morning, Ms. Richmond," the girl answered without raising her eyes from the unbelievably long nail she was manicuring. "But Mrs. Downing is waiting to see you."

"Okay. Give me about five minutes, then send Mrs. Downing in."

By the time she had checked on her phone messages and emptied out her briefcase, the attractive blonde was being led into Jan's office by her secretary, Barbra.

"This is Carole Downing, Ms. Richmond."

"Good morning, Mrs. Downing." Jan extended her hand to the woman and was pleased when her handshake was firmly returned. "I'm Janelle Richmond,

Mr. Whitmann's associate, and I'll be handling your case, if that's satisfactory with you."

The interview lasted over an hour, at least fifteen minutes more than Jan had allowed for in her busy schedule. She found that she was fascinated by the ramifications of Carole Downing's case, and she couldn't wait to thank Mark for giving her the opportunity to work on it.

Carole Downing was a thirty-six-year-old woman who had married young, borne two children, and been a model wife and mother for almost twelve years. Then one morning Carole had awakened with the desire to do something more. She had returned to college the next semester, taken an arts' degree, and within another year, she had opened her own interior-design studio. Carole's husband, John, had been furious. He accused Carole of neglecting him and their children. Carole could not understand John's attitude and his lack of understanding about her needs. Finally, the couple agreed to a divorce. Carole was granted permanent custody of their children, John, Jr., age twelve, and Melissa, age ten. Now, two years after the divorce decree was granted, John had remarried and was instituting a suit for custody of Johnny and Missy, on the grounds that Carole was an unfit mother.

John's petition for custody charged that Carole worked excessively long hours and dated frequently, leaving the children under the care of a baby-sitter and/or housekeeper, that she devoted very little time to their emotional or physical needs, and further alleged "that she is keeping company with unsavory characters known to have low moral standards, which persons are not fit companions for the said minors."

Every time Jan reread that paragraph of the petition, she saw red. Carole was a lovely person who really cared for her children and was doing her best to raise them without a father. She worked long hours on her job because it was necessary to build up her clientele and firmly establish herself in a very competitive business. She dated only two or three times a month, and she swore to Jan that even then she usually telephoned the children during her absence and rushed home early to be with them.

Jan considered the institution of the suit for custody to be a cruel, inhuman act on the part of Carole's ex-husband and she suspected that there was much more at stake here than the custody of two children. What were really at stake were Carole's rights as a woman. And Jan intended to protect those rights, if it took every ounce of legal expertise she possessed.

After Carole left the office, Jan swiveled her chair around so that she could look out through the tall window behind the desk. She sat there for a long time, pondering Carole's future and her own.

In spite of the fact that her profession usually magnified the bad side of marriage in domestic battles, Jan had always firmly believed that two people could be happily married and remain so throughout their lives. Her own parents were proof enough of that; her mom and dad were so satisfied with each other's company, even after thirty years of marriage, that they didn't seem to need anyone else. Not even their only daughter. Jan had resented their relationship when she was younger, feeling that her presence in her parents' home was nothing more than an intrusion into their private world. But that was before she grew up and began to understand how really special her parents' marriage was. Studying law and later practicing it, Jan had been rapidly disillusioned by divorce statistics and literally sickened by the way love could turn to disinterest or hatred in the span of a few short years.

The Downing case was a perfect example. Jan asked herself over and over again why a man like John Downing, a man who had been comfortably married for twelve years, would suddenly become so dissatisfied with his life? Was it really because of Carole's blossoming career, or was it simply that he had tired of her and was using her new life-style as an excuse to get out of a marriage that had gone stale? Jan wished she knew the answer to that question. It would certainly make it easier to represent Carole. And to be honest with herself, she had personal reasons for wanting to know the answer.

Blair Wynter. She said his name aloud, enjoying the sound of it on her lips. When she closed her eyes, Jan could envision every aspect of his face: the broad forehead and high cheekbones, the strong jaw line, the tiny smile lines at the corners of his extraordinary eyes. Finally, she had met a man who interested her, who *challenged* her. She was sure Blair Wynter was a man who could invoke her emotions and fire her desires. Now Jan was looking at marriage and divorce from a different prospective.

As a lawyer who handled more than her share of divorce and custody cases, Jan suddenly found herself dredging up her old ideals and looking for a flaw in the statistics. After all, statistics were only numbers on paper. They said nothing about the illusive thing called love, and what part love played in keeping a couple together, against all the odds.

Jan stared out her window at the darkening late-afternoon sky and wondered if it was too much to ask that the odds fall in her favor.

Chapter Two

❧

Jan was awake at six, but she didn't get out of bed until the strains of a popular love song softly echoed from her clock radio, signaling that it was six-forty-five. She had been thinking about Blair Wynter since the moment she awoke, and she was again experiencing that tingling sense of anticipation she had felt when they were running side by side in the park.

She padded across the thick white shag carpeting in her bare feet and started the shower running in the bathroom. Back in the bedroom, she shed her lime-green pajamas and assessed her reflection in the full-length mirror. This morning she was especially thankful for her sensible eating habits and the sporadic running that helped keep her in shape.

After her shower, she rummaged back and forth through her ample closet, wondering what in the world you wear to breakfast with a man you hardly know. Especially when you know *he'll* be wearing a sweaty jogging suit. Finally, she settled for a casual outfit of beige wool slacks and a matching cashmere cardigan over a pale honey-colored shirt. Luckily, she had a skirt the same color as the slacks that she could easily change into before she left for the office. She used the blow-dryer on her hair, then brushed it out and let it hang in soft waves to her shoulders. Jan considered her shiny, long brown hair to be one of her most attractive features and she knew that it was shown off to best advantage when she did very little to it.

She left her apartment shortly before eight, giving herself just enough time to cut across the park to the restaurant. Her heart jumped in her chest when she spotted Blair waiting for her in front of the restaurant. He was so incredibly attractive. As she had anticipated, he was wearing a jogging suit, and when she got closer to him, she could see that he'd been running. Jan's pulse quickened as she approached him, and when he turned his head toward her, she felt giddy and light-headed.

"Good morning, Blair."

"Good morning," he answered. "You look great." His green eyes gave her slim figure an appreciative once-over and returned to her face. She blushed furiously, but refused to look away from his compelling eyes. "I'm afraid I lost track of time. I intended to run home and change, but eight o'clock sort of crept up on me."

"You'll do." Jan laughed. "Actually, I doubt if I'd recognize you dressed any other way."

Blair casually took her arm as though he had been doing it all his life, but to Jan the contact was anything but casual. She could feel his strong fingers gripping her arm through the soft fabric of her sweater, burning into her tender flesh. Her arm tingled again, as it had when she'd shaken his hand in the park, and she wondered if he would always have this kind of an effect on her.

"Well, you're going to be sorry you invited me to breakfast. This is when I eat my biggest meal of the day. Jogging before breakfast gives me what you might call a hearty appetite."

Inside the restaurant, Blair proved that he hadn't been joking about his appetite. While Jan ate a thin slice of melon and sipped a cup of black coffee, he put away an order of ham and eggs with biscuits and a large glass of orange juice.

"Now you know why I run every day," he said, patting his flat stomach. "If I stopped running, I could probably gain fifty pounds without even trying."

"That's rather hard to imagine." Jan laughed, unable to picture him as anything but perfect. Her eyes drank in his physical perfection, lingering on the broad expanse of his shoulders that strained the fabric of his running jacket. She had a strong desire to stretch out her hands, to touch the taut muscles of his arms. She knew how his arms would feel, the skin velvety soft, the muscle hard as iron. She folded her hands in her lap and forced herself to concentrate on what he was saying.

"Don't laugh," he told her. "I was a fat little kid. In the sixth grade, all the little girls laughed at me and called me 'Chubby.' "

"I can't imagine that either."

"No?" His brows arched questioningly over his green eyes.

"No," Jan said firmly. "I'll bet you were the Don Juan of the sixth grade. Tying knots in their pigtails, carrying their school books."

"Go on," he urged.

"Am I right so far?"

"Right on target."

"Then I can see you walking them home from school, stealing a quick kiss before you ran away. I imagine you were quite a runner, even then."

"I never ran away. And I'll bet you didn't either." His voice was low and intimate and suddenly it wasn't the sixth grade they were discussing. They were still sitting on opposite sides of the table, but when their eyes met and held, the impact was as strong as a physical contact. Jan felt a soft film of perspiration break out across her brow and a subtle warmth envelop her. It felt as though someone had turned the heat up a notch too high.

Blair tugged at the zipper of his navy jogging jacket and pulled it down from his throat just enough to give him some air.

"Warm in here, isn't it?"

"Yes," Jan murmured, fully aware that he wasn't talking about the temperature in the room.

Don't let this happen so fast, an inner voice cautioned her. Keep it slow and easy. Slow and easy . . . like his smile.

Jan was grateful when their waitress approached the table with a fresh pot of coffee. She eagerly held out her cup for a refill and Blair did the same.

"What do you do for a living, Jan?" Blair asked after the waitress had filled their cups and left them alone again.

"I'm a lawyer," she answered, after only a second's hesitation. She had been hoping he wouldn't ask, but she didn't want to lie to him now that he had.

"A lawyer?" Once more he raised his brows over his cool green eyes and looked at her in disbelief.

"That's right," she answered almost defensively. "And you?"

"I guess you could say we're colleagues."

"*You're* a lawyer?" She had to smile at the thought of him in a suit and tie. There was something wrong with the picture. Was there a standard jacket size made to fit those wide shoulders?

"Do you find that amusing?" he asked, sounding not at all amused.

"Oh, no!" she hastened to assure him. "It's just that—"

"You think of me as more the construction-worker type?" he volunteered.

"Well . . ."

"I think I'll take that as a positive comment on my physical condition rather than a negative one on my mental abilities."

"That was exactly how I meant it," Jan answered quickly, her dark-blue eyes dancing with amusement.

"What firm is lucky enough to have your considerable talents at their disposal?" Blair asked.

"I've been with Babcock, Wynne and Whitmann since I got out of school. Mark Whitmann is an old friend of my father's. They went to school together. But that's not why he hired me," she added quickly. "Mark isn't like that. He's—"

"Hey, I believe you," Blair told her, still smiling that maddening smile. "I've met Mark. He's a damned good attorney."

"Do you have your own practice?" Jan asked, to get the subject away from herself. She thought the answer would be yes. She couldn't imagine Blair Wynter taking orders from anyone, or selling himself short in the name of security either. And, of course, the main reason for working for one of the big law firms (or a small, well-known firm with a good name) was the steady paycheck every week, whether business was good or bad. His answer surprised her.

"No," he answered slowly, "I'm Stu Underwood's latest fair-haired boy, but not for long. I want to see my own name engraved at the top of my own firm's letterhead."

"What made you go to work for a man like Stu Underwood?" Jan asked. "I mean, he's a *very* good lawyer, but he has the reputation of being extremely hard to work for."

"Oh, Stu's okay," Blair answered easily, "and until I can afford to open my own office I'd rather work for him than join one of the bigger firms."

"Why is that?" Jan asked, sincerely interested.

"Frankly, I'm hoping some of Stu's genius will rub off on me. It seems to me that once you join one of the bigger firms, you kind of get lost in the shuffle. With Stu, I'm getting a lot of exposure and getting a chance to handle different types of cases."

"What about your caseload? Does Stu assign you so many cases per month to handle on your own?" Jan asked.

"Of course, I have a few of my own cases. But Stu likes for me to know a little bit about every file that passes through the office. That way I can cover for him if he can't make a hearing or a meeting."

"But that isn't fair. That way, very few cases are ever really *yours*. Everything you do, you do in the name of Stu Underwood. It must be very frustrating."

"Is it any different at Wynne, Babcock?" Blair's voice had an edge to it, and she realized she had gone too far in her insinuation that she was working for a better firm than his. She knew she was only being defensive because of her doubts about her own job, but she also realized Blair had no way of knowing that.

"Yes, it is different," she answered truthfully, but in a gentle voice she hoped would make up for her offense. "Mark assigns the cases when they first come into the office. The junior partners get an even share of the caseload. Then one of the senior partners might sit in on a conference or offer some advice as to how a case should be handled, but basically, once a case is assigned to me, it belongs to me."

"You don't get a choice of cases, though," Blair said. "And you don't get a chance to handle any of the really big cases. I know how that system works— junior partners get all the 'nuisance cases,' while anything that might get your name in the papers is reserved for a senior partner."

"True," Jan answered, "but that's only because they have more experience. Anyway, if I stayed with Mark, I'd be in line for a senior partnership in a few more years. Then I'd have my choice of cases."

"Still, it's one hell of a way to run an office, if you ask me. The class system. At least I feel as if I'm Stu's equal in the practice, even if I don't share equally in the revenues."

"Well, I guess both systems have their good points," Jan offered by way of appeasement. "Of course, the best system of all is to have your own practice."

"That's something we agree on. I noticed you said *if* you stayed with Mark you'd be in line for a senior partnership. Does that mean you're not planning on staying with him?"

"I've always dreamed of opening my own office, ever since I first became interested in law. I hope it won't be too much longer before I can make that dream come true."

"If that's what you want, then I hope you make it," Blair said. "Do you want to specialize when you're on your own, or do you plan on being one of those old-fashioned 'general practitioners'?"

"I want to specialize in divorce and custody law. And if the case I'm now working on meets my expectations, it may not be too much longer before I can make the break."

"Divorce and custody law would bore the hell out of me," Blair admitted. "Of course, I handle those cases when Stu takes them on."

"Well, don't keep me in suspense. What *do* you intend to specialize in?"

"Oh, corporate law probably."

"It seems to me you'd have to deal with a lot of crooked people to practice corporate law," Jan said. "How will you know the bad guys from the good guys?"

"The good guys always wear white hats, didn't you know that?" Blair joked. "But seriously, I wouldn't be going into that type of practice to protect the innocent. You build a reputation by winning your cases, not by what side you're on."

"Well, maybe you could live with that. I couldn't," Jan said.

"And what would you do, Miss Richmond, have your prospective clients swear their innocence on a stack of Bibles before you took them on?" Blair asked, his green eyes dancing with amusement.

"I don't think that would be necessary," Jan answered indignantly. "I think I'm a pretty fair judge of character."

Blair looked as if he would like to carry the conversation further, but he apparently thought better of it, and Jan was glad. They were getting into territory where it would be necessary to either fight each other or compromise, and she didn't think Blair Wynter was much of a compromiser. For that matter, neither was she.

But in spite of their disagreements, Jan was inordinately pleased that she and Blair shared not only a common profession, but a common dream as well. It seemed that being independent and owning their own offices was uppermost in both their minds. She couldn't remember a time when she had not had the dream, and now she had someone to share it with.

"Well, Janelle Richmond," Blair said, expertly turning the conversation away from controversy, "I'll bet you're one hell of a good lawyer. I hope I never have to come up against you in court." He leaned toward her across the narrow table that separated them.

Taking a deep breath, Jan inhaled the scent of the autumn morning that clung to him.

"But," Blair went on, "speaking of coming up against you ..." He lowered his voice to an intimate whisper. "I'd like that very much."

"Keep it clean, Blair," Jan answered glibly, doing her best to hide her discomfort, "this is a family restaurant."

He laughed and leaned back in his chair again, never taking his eyes from her face. "I just happen to know the chef at a little French place in the Village. The man is a genius, makes the best boeuf bourguignon in the city of New York. And Chez François is definitely *not* a family restaurant."

"Are you asking me for a date, in your rather roundabout way?"

"Just offering to repay your generosity." He waved his hand to take in the empty breakfast dishes. "I never like to be indebted to a lady."

"Well?" he prompted when Jan didn't respond immediately.

"How could I refuse such a gracious offer?"

"Tonight?"

"Tonight is fine."

He glanced at his watch and automatically reached for his wallet as he signaled their waitress for the check.

"Uh-uh," Jan cautioned, opening her bag and extracting several bills. "My treat, remember?"

He walked her through the park and left her at the door to her apartment building with a reminder that he would pick her up around eight-thirty. He didn't try to touch her, but several times his arm lightly brushed hers as they walked, sending small shivers of pleasure through her body.

During the course of their walk, Jan learned that Blair was thirty-four years old, and a more or less confirmed bachelor.

"I almost took the plunge once, a long time ago," he confided.

"What happened?" Jan wasn't entirely sure she wanted to know.

"It just didn't work out. I'm still not sure why I got cold feet. Maybe I just wasn't ready to give up my freedom. How about you?"

"Twenty-nine and still single."

"Why?"

"Does it sound too hackneyed to say that I'm still waiting for the right man to come along?" Jan asked.

Blair laughed and gave her long, lean body a slow appraisal before he replied. "I'm not sure I believe you, but we'll let it pass for now."

Jan was only too glad to let the question pass. She didn't feel up to trying to explain her true feelings to a man who was still virtually a stranger. How could she explain to him that she placed a high value on her complete womanhood, on the combination of her femininity, her sexuality, and her intellect. That she didn't want to sacrifice even a small part of herself for a relationship. Would he understand that that was exactly what most men seemed to expect of her, that she would magically change into their preconceived conception of the ideal woman the minute they proposed a lasting relationship? Was that what *he* would expect?

Chez François was everything Blair had promised, and it definitely was *not* a family restaurant. There was an air of quiet sensuality about the place, which was filled with couples sitting close together at tiny white-clothed tables, talking intimately.

Jan and Blair were sitting on a small balcony, at a table barely large enough to hold two elegantly plain place settings and a fresh red rose in a crystal vase. The menu, which was about half the size of their table, was printed in French.

"This is lovely, Blair," Jan told him as she glanced around the room. "And I didn't even know it existed."

"François doesn't advertise," Blair answered. "He gets more business than he can handle from word-of-mouth referrals. So unless you know someone who's been here, you probably wouldn't know about it."

"Well, I'm glad I finally met someone who's been here before."

"So am I."

He smiled warmly and Jan thought he looked especially handsome in his dark-gray suit, which he had complimented with a dove-gray silk shirt and a striped tie that added blue to several shades of gray. She could hardly believe the way he looked in a suit—trim and sophisticated and urbane. If she had met him when he was dressed like this, she probably wouldn't have been able to envision him in ragged jogging clothes.

His sandy hair looked lighter than she remembered it, and his green eyes were so clear that she imagined she could see right through them.

"To us." Blair's deep voice broke into her thoughts. He lifted his goblet of white wine and clinked it gently against hers.

"To us." Jan echoed his words as she took a sip of the delicate, fragrant wine.

She saw that Blair was watching her appreciatively, and she was glad that she had worn the new burgundy silk dress. The color complimented her creamy white skin and the soft, clinging material did wonders for her figure. The dress was cut high in the front, then dipped in the back, exposing her smooth, soft skin to the waist. Wearing it, she felt wickedly sensuous and completely feminine.

When they had entered the restaurant, Blair had checked her shawl, then casually guided her into the darkened dining room. The touch of his hand on her bare back had generated heat through her entire body and Jan found herself wishing that they could forget about dinner and go somewhere to dance the evening away, so that she could continue to feel his beautiful, strong hands on her body.

Even sitting across from him at the small table, she could actually feel his presence, and she looked forward with pleasure to his next touch. They shared an easy intimacy as their conversation ranged over a variety of subjects. We get along like old friends, Jan thought. Or new lovers.

With Jan's consent, Blair ordered the boeuf bourguignon for two, and it proved to be the best she had ever eaten. The succulent beef almost melted in her mouth, and the vegetables were heavenly. For dessert, they had lighter-than-air French pastries and espresso coffee.

"That may well have been the best meal I've ever eaten," Jan commented to the owner/chef when he

stopped by their table. "Everything Blair says about
you is true."

"Blair is a true connoisseur of French cuisine,"
François answered, obviously pleased, "so I will accept humbly your compliment. He is also a connoisseur of beautiful women, and you are certainly the
most beautiful woman to grace Chez François this
night."

"Thank you," Jan murmured, not at all embarrassed, since she was sure that flowery speech and
excessive flattery were an accepted part of the charm
of Chez François and its owner.

When François left them, Blair reached for her
hand across the table. "He's right, you know. You
are the most beautiful woman here tonight."

"And you are the most handsome man," she
answered, nestling her hand in his and returning his
admiring gaze.

Still holding on to her hand, Blair signaled their
waiter for the check and reached for his wallet with
his free hand.

"What are you smiling about?" he asked when he
had skillfully extracted several bills and replaced
the wallet in his pocket without once releasing Jan's
hand.

"You," she answered. "You're very good at that."
She indicated the pile of money resting on top of
the check.

"I'm very good at everything I do." He gave her
hand a light tug and she responded automatically,
leaning toward him until his lips met hers and
brushed them gently. Just as quickly, she leaned
back in her chair, her head spinning from the nearness
of Blair Wynter, who made her feel like a teenager in
love for the very first time.

* * *

Later, on the way home, they decided it was a beautiful night for a romantic walk in the moonlight. They left Blair's car in the garage beneath his apartment building, which was only a few blocks from Jan's building. She found it hard to believe that they had lived so close together and worked at the same profession for years without ever having met before.

The night was chilly, with a hint of winter in the cool, dry air. They both agreed that fall is the best time of the year in New York. A thin slice of yellow moon floated high above the city skyline and the night sky was dotted with a thousand twinkling stars. After swapping a few law-school stories, they fell silent, enjoying each other and the relative peacefulness of the night.

When they reached Jan's building, they stopped in the shadows beside the door. Blair put both hands on her shoulders and turned Jan to face him, the night and his touch fanning the flame that had smoldered in their hearts and bodies since their first meeting. He gently touched her lips with his, and another lick of flame leaped between them, hinting at hidden fires of passion.

"Let me come upstairs with you," Blair whispered hoarsely.

Jan shook her head slowly and fought the pull of his magnetic green eyes. "Not tonight, Blair. This is all happening too fast for me."

"Are you trying to tell me you're an old-fashioned girl?" He held her at arm's length and studied her face, as though he was trying to commit every detail of her loveliness to memory.

"No, I'm not old-fashioned. But I don't live completely by impulse either. We hardly know each other."

"I think we know each other better than you'd like to admit."

He pulled Jan into his arms and pressed her softness against the hard planes of his muscular body. Only his lips were soft as they planted light kisses down her cheek, onto her neck and her bare shoulders. She shivered with pleasure and, for just a moment, considered giving in, as she imagined what it would be like to surrender completely. The thought of his lips continuing down the length of her body sparked an almost irresistible desire that she fought to control. She wanted only to lie down beside him, to give in to her emotions and follow this thing that they had started through to its natural ending. She knew that it would be right to surrender her body to his hands and his lips, to let herself become one with him. And she was almost sure that it couldn't be for one night, not if he was feeling even half of the desire that was coursing through her body. But the very strength of her physical desire unnerved Jan and made her back down. She had to admit to herself that she was actually afraid of the way her body was responding to this man she hardly knew.

With a deep sense of loss, she stepped out of Blair's arms and reached into her tiny black bag, extracting the key to her apartment.

"Good night, Blair," she said firmly. "And thank you for a lovely evening."

"My pleasure," he answered as he released her with clear reluctance.

She waited inside the door and watched him move out of the circle of light that held him, half-hoping that he would come back and break down the weak barrier of her resistance. But his shadow quickly melded with the darker shadows of the night and he was gone.

Alone in her apartment, Jan realized that Blair hadn't said that he would see her again or even mentioned that he would call. She was devastated by the thought that she might have lost him . . . that he had actually been interested in a one-night stand. She had refused him—and he was gone.

It took her a long time to fall asleep, and when she finally slept, Jan's elusive dreams fell just short of being nightmares.

Chapter Three

In the morning, Jan awakened to a gray, cheerless room and the depressing sight of rain running in wide rivulets down her bedroom windowpane. As quickly as the thought of Blair Wynter warmed her, the thought of his possible defection turned the blood in her veins to ice water. She shuddered as she made her way to the bathroom, hugging herself for warmth.

You're wrong, she told herself repeatedly. Just because he didn't say he'll call doesn't mean he won't. Any minute now, the phone will ring. Any minute now. But minutes stretched into slow-moving hours and the phone became a silent reminder of what she had let slip through her fingers.

Jan dressed in a pale-yellow linen dress that she seldom wore to the office, hoping that it would cheer her up, but it didn't work. It was a day when everything she touched turned sour. She spent hours working on a complicated trust agreement, only to receive a telephone call that the parties involved had "changed their minds." She had an argument with one of the law clerks over some important research that he had "forgotten" she'd ordered. And when her secretary, Barbra, came in to ask if there was anything wrong, Jan almost burst into tears.

At four o'clock, she decided to give up and go home early. She left orders with Barbra that she would be "out of town" to anyone except Mark and a couple of other lawyers, including Blair Wynter.

She hadn't told Mark she was leaving, since he would surely fuss over her and treat her headache as if it were a major illness. Mark had promised her father that he would take care of her and he certainly couldn't be faulted for failing to keep his word.

She had just pushed the button for the elevator when Mark emerged from the dark wood and leather cocoon of his office. He was dressed impeccably in a custom-tailored navy suit, and there wasn't a silver gray hair out of place on his head. There were a lot of women around who wouldn't mind being the second Mrs. Mark Whitmann, Jan thought proudly as she watched him walk toward her.

"Janelle," he called out in greeting, raising his hand and smiling warmly.

"Oh, Mark—I didn't know you were in."

"We just finished off the Gianelli case. I'm anxious to tell you about it. Where in the world are you rushing off to at this hour?" Mark had suddenly realized that she was on her way out, not just passing time in front of the elevator.

"I'd love to hear how you handled the case, Mark, but could I take a raincheck? I was just going to sneak out and head for home."

"You don't look well, Janelle. Are you ill?" Mark placed a cool, manicured hand across her forehead and frowned dramatically. "You are a little warm, darling."

"It's just a headache, Mark. But I would like to call it a day, if you don't mind."

"Of course, of course." He pressed the elevator button and fussed with the collar of her tan London Fog. "I won't have you riding the subways in this weather, Janelle. You can flag a taxicab right in front of the building. Do you have the fare?"

"Of course, I do, Mark." Jan couldn't help but smile, in spite of her headache. Her salary as a junior partner was very generous, but it was so like Mark to offer her cab fare.

After minutes that passed like hours, the elevator doors opened and Jan stepped in.

"Shall I give you a call later this evening to see how you're feeling?" Mark was holding the elevator doors open with his hand.

"I think I'll try to get some sleep as soon as I get home. When I wake up, I'll call you. Okay?"

"Good girl." Mark finally released the elevator doors, but, even as they closed and she descended, Jan could hear his voice: "You're probably coming down with a bug, Janelle. Drink some hot tea with fresh lemon juice before you go to bed."

The irony of it was that it turned out she *was* coming down with something. And the state of her health was at least partially responsible for what she referred to as "D-Day," for disaster day.

The next morning she woke up with a sore throat and a slight fever and was pathetically relieved to find out that she was ill and not losing her sanity over Blair Wynter. At nine she called the office and told Mark that she wouldn't be in, finally convincing him that she didn't need to see a doctor.

It was a Friday and Mark suggested that she stay in bed for the weekend, drink plenty of liquids, and call him if she needed anything that the drugstore couldn't or wouldn't deliver. Jan gratefully accepted his prescription and agreed to follow his advice, at least for the remainder of the day.

She passed the day sleeping fitfully and, in her wakeful interludes, reading a new paperback novel that she had picked up at the drugstore when she stopped to buy medication for her headache on her way home the night before. At least, she *tried* to read. And she tried not to think about Blair Wynter, although she didn't have much success in denying him entrance into her mind.

He's not going to call, she finally admitted to herself. I might as well face it, the evening didn't mean that much to him. Not as much as it meant to me. I thought it might be the beginning of something wonderful, but that kind of a relationship takes two. Obviously, Blair Wynter and I weren't looking for the same thing. Tears welled up in her eyes and she angrily swiped at them with the back of her hand and blamed her running eyes on her "bug" and her despondency on low metabolism.

When the sun set on Friday, Jan knew that the worst was over. She had always been known for her remarkable recuperative powers. "Janelle Richmond, the rubber lady. She can bounce back from anything." But she wasn't smiling as she said it.

After another restless night, Saturday dawned clear and sunny. The rain had gone, leaving Jan's little corner of the city fresh and clean in its aftermath. She was determined to match her mood to the weather, although her head was still stuffy and her throat still a little raw. She spent ten minutes in the shower, scrubbing away at the last vestiges of self-pity before she climbed into a pair of faded jeans and pulled an old flannel shirt from the back of her closet. The large shirt was a leftover from her father's last visit to New York several years before. He had inadvertently left the shirt behind and Jan had never gotten around to sending it to him. The truth was that she liked to wear it now and then because, no matter how many times the shirt was laundered, she imagined that her father's special familiar scent lingered in the soft, warm fabric.

She didn't examine her motives for wearing the shirt on this particular day, she only knew that it made her feel good. Today, that was reason enough.

She plaited her long hair into one thick braid and let it fall heavily across her shoulder. With her face scrubbed free of makeup, she looked younger than her twenty-nine years. Young and soft and vulnerable. Only the dark circles beneath her eyes reminded her that she had spent two nearly sleepless nights since her last encounter with Blair Wynter.

For a fleeting moment, she wondered if she dared leave the security of her apartment for the open spaces of the park, where she was far too likely to run into him again. Then she made a face at her solemn reflection in the bathroom mirror and ran out of the apartment quickly, before she had time to change her mind.

There were several runners in the park but none that even vaguely resembled Blair. None that exhibited even half his grace or style, none that moved her. Jan ran listlessly around the track, which was still muddy and puddled from the recent rain. The course seemed endlessly long and she felt, at several points, that she would never be able to finish it. Her legs were leaden and heavy, her arms and shoulders tired and aching.

Finally, after what seemed like hours of running, she gratefully sighted the end of her course. She left the park with a mixture of pride that she had run in spite of her cold, and relief that the run was over and she could return to the warmth and security of her apartment.

Upon reaching the wide street that separated her apartment building from the park, she stopped cold. Along one side of her building there was a low brick wall that enclosed a decorative miniature rock garden. Blair Wynter was sitting on that wall, elbows on knees, chin resting in the cup of his hands. His face was turned away from Jan, but there was no mistaking that body or the mop of sandy hair that fell over his face.

On legs that seemed to be the consistency of warm marshmallows, Jan crossed with the light and approached the wall until she stood within two or three feet of the brooding, statue-still man.

"Blair?" It was one word that asked everything she needed so desperately to know. Is it really you, Blair? Are you here because you couldn't stay away? Why did you let me spend two awful days and nights wondering if it was over between us almost before it had begun?

He slowly swiveled his head toward her, as if he couldn't be sure that he had actually heard her voice.

"Jan!" In a single movement he was standing beside her, wrapping her in his arms, bending his fair head to hers. Her lips opened like blossoms seeking the sun, and when he kissed her, she knew that everything was right between them.

"Oh, dear God, how I've missed you, Jan," he murmured as he bit gently on the perfect shell of her ear and nuzzled the smooth column of her throat.

"Why didn't you call?" she had to ask when she found her voice again.

"Oh, Jan, I'm sorry. I had it all planned—I was going to wake you in the morning with the musical sound of my voice. I wanted to prove to you that I wanted more than a one-night stand. I went to sleep thinking about you, I dreamed about you. Then Stu Underwood woke me up at five A.M. with the news that I had to fly to Washington in his place. He'd come down with some kind of a flu bug that's going around. Hey, why are you laughing? It wasn't exactly funny at the time. I barely had time to make my flight and we were so busy in D.C. that it was almost midnight before I could relax and get a minute to myself."

"It's all right," Jan reassured him, weak with relief that something as simple as a flu epidemic had kept them apart. "It doesn't matter now. You're here, that's all that matters."

As they kissed again and clung to each other hungrily, they began to attract the attention of several passersby.

"I think we'd better go upstairs," Jan said, pulling herself out of his arms.

"Are you sure, Jan?" His green eyes shone with a feverish light and his voice was hoarse with desire for her, but it was obvious that he wanted her only if she was ready.

"I'm sure," Jan answered as she took his hand and led him into the building.

In the elevator, Blair put his arm around Jan's slim waist and pulled her close to him. She could feel the heat of his body and the rapid, strong beat of his heart through his jacket. The way he held her so possessively in his powerful arms sent her blood singing through her veins as the elevator made its way slowly upward.

Jan's fingers could have been made of ice, the way they froze up and fumbled with the key to her apartment. Finally, Blair took the key from her hand and deftly inserted it into the lock. As the door swung closed behind them, Blair took Jan's shoulders and turned her into his arms. She tilted her head to receive his lips, which briefly and softly touched the corners of her mouth. Then, surprising herself, she hungrily sought the fullness of his mouth, pressing her lips to his, gently slipping her tongue between his teeth.

She felt as if she were on a roller coaster, dropping through the sky, dizzy with an unfulfilled desire that was new to her, yet somehow familiar.

When she opened her eyes, Blair's beautiful green gaze burned into hers, and Jan could see the surprise registered there.

She smilingly led him down the hallway to her bedroom, her heart pounding wildly in her chest. Her fingers trembled as she pushed his jacket from his wide shoulders. Not a word passed between them, but Blair's narrowed eyes spoke volumes as he watched Jan undo the three small buttons at the neckline of his shirt and then tug it over his head. She buried her face against his naked chest and opened her mouth to drink in the taste of his skin, still cool from the fall morning.

She marveled in the feel of his naked chest beneath her hands. It was smooth and deeply tanned, with a sprinkling of golden hairs. She ran her hands down his chest to the top of his jogging pants and felt the hard muscles of his stomach under her searching fingertips.

Blair responded by running the palms of his hands gently up and down her back in a slow caressing motion. His chest rose and fell rapidly, as he removed her shirt and then fumbled with the catch of her bra. Jan reached back to help him free her small, perfect breasts, and then he touched her, lowering his head to take her nipples gently into his mouth. The touch of his lips on her sensitive skin brought a gasp of pleasure to Jan's lips, as she realized how she had been waiting for this moment, longing for it, silently willing him to touch her this way.

He kissed her smooth shoulders and the hollow of her throat as he murmured her name and whispered his need for her. Then his hands found the ribbon that held her mane of dark hair. When he had removed it, he ran his fingers through the braid and freed her mass of hair to flow across her naked shoulders. "Beautiful," he murmured as he buried his face in her fragrant hair and inhaled its sweet scent.

Weak with desire, Jan quickly shed the rest of her clothes.

Blair was clearly mesmerized by the sight of her long legs, her full hips and her slender, tapering waist. As soon as she stepped out of her bikinis, he took the step that closed the space between them and swept her up in his arms.

"I have never wanted a woman so much before," he whispered into her hair. "You believe that, don't you?"

"Yes," Jan whispered back. "I believe that."

Blair lowered her to the pale-blue sheets and knelt beside the bed. Jan clung to him and ran her tongue across his chest, wishing that she could hold on to this moment of near-perfect awareness when they were not quite lovers, yet knew that they soon would be. Then, as her mouth sought his, her hands reached to untie the cord of his jogging pants. He stood to step out of them, and Jan felt a thrill of pleasure at the sight of his hard, lean body. He was perfect, or as close to perfection as a man could ever be. His long legs with their well-muscled thighs, his flat stomach, his smooth golden chest.

This man will be my lover, she thought, and the overused word took on a new meaning as she applied it to Blair Wynter. He will be my lover in every sense of the word. Because she knew that loving Blair with her body would be only part of loving him. Maybe the most pleasurable part, but surely not the most important part. Because she wanted to love Blair Wynter with her whole heart and soul. She wanted to love him forever, and she knew that today was only the beginning.

His eyes drank in her loveliness as he asked, "Do you really want me as much as I want you, my darling?"

His words were music to Jan's ears, a melody that sent blood racing through her body in glad response.

"Oh, hurry," she murmured, and he bent over her, running his tongue down her flat stomach, down the outside of her silken thighs and up again. "You're so perfect," he whispered urgently, and again Jan felt a tug of fear that this man could make her body answer his so completely.

Her eyes closed dreamily and her body came alive to the touch of his hands and his mouth. Somehow, he found a way to ignite her deepest wells of desire and bring them to flame.

"Perfect," he insisted, and his words tingled against her body as his lips continued to work their magic.

"Oh, Blair," Jan cried out, feeling that she was about to lose the last vestige of her control. She rested her head against his chest and nipped at the golden hairs. He tasted salty/sweet like nothing she had ever known before. As his tongue moved to the center of her silken thighs, Jan arched her back and cried out with unrestrained joy. The tension that had built in her body snapped and melted into warm release.

Blair's eyes lingered on her lovely face as he climbed onto the bed and straddled her body. "You are the most perfect, complete woman I've ever known," he said, shaking his head in wonderment. "It's worth everything to be able to bring that look to your face."

"Don't talk," Jan begged, "just love me."

His warm lips touched her smooth shoulders, lingering only long enough to gather the taste of her in his mouth. Then slowly he moved his lips to her alabaster breasts, and his tongue was an instrument of magic as he licked at her nipples and sucked them to exquisite, swollen peaks.

Jan's entire body throbbed with desire for him. Her head swam as he raised his mouth to taste her lips, then moved them slowly back down her sleek body, seeking to savor every part of her. She let her hands roam across his wide shoulders, and she exulted in the strength that waited just beneath the surface of his taut flesh. The muscles of his arms were powerful, his back wide and smooth. Tentatively, Jan's fingers traced the curve of his hips and the flat planes of his stomach.

When he bent his head to taste again the honey of her silken center, Jan wound her fingers in his sandy hair and moaned softly. His tongue darted and teased and she gripped his shoulders and dug her fingernails into his flesh.

Sweet fire bubbled in her veins and burst forth in white-hot need for him. She knew the pent-up emotions of the past few days would soon find sweet release, and she arched her body and wordlessly begged him to take her fully.

Jan's desire kindled Blair's own, and she felt heady with power when she realized the extent of his need, every bit as urgent as her own. Finally, he was no longer able to hold back. He lowered his long body onto hers and she wound her arms around his neck to pull him even closer. She moved her legs beneath his, conscious of the soft hair and the hard muscle of his legs. She wriggled her body and pressed the tips of her breasts against his chest, touched every part of him, as he kissed her again, slowly caressed her swollen lips with his. His hand covered her narrow waist, then moved upward to tug gently at her erect nipples, and a sweeping wave of desire engulfed her. Then his hand moved slowly downward until he was caressing her flat stomach, moving tantalizingly closer to the part of her that so longed for his touch. But when he finally moved his hand to touch her there, she found that it wasn't enough. She burned to have him inside of her, to become one with him.

She pressed her hands against his strong, hard back, then down over his rounded buttocks. He once again whispered of his need for her and his voice was throaty and deeper than ever.

How much longer can he stand this sweet ecstasy? How much longer could she sustain this wild pitch of desire that had now spread to every part of her body? She felt as though her nerves had been scraped raw, wound into a tight coil that strained for release.

Then, suddenly, he moved between her thighs and entered her in one graceful, flowing motion. He moved slowly at first, then faster and faster above her, in a rhythm as old as mankind but as new as her desire for him. She sang out his name as she sought to press his flesh ever closer to her own and he continued to stoke the fires of their passion.

Jan's breasts were sensitive, her belly and the insides of her thighs ached, but there was no pain, only an ecstatic climbing toward the highest peak of pleasure she had ever known.

Blair moved faster above her. His hands rested on her shoulders, his chest crushed her own, his lips murmured her name over and over again. Suddenly Jan tensed her muscles, then relaxed and gave herself up to a rocking spasm of ecstasy. She heard a voice that seemed strangely detached from her body murmuring Blair's name over and over, a litany of love, as wave after shuddering wave of pleasure pounded through her body. Then he, too, cried out as he found fulfillment.

Finally, limp and drained, Jan twined her slim legs around Blair's and rolled with him until they lay on their sides, bodies touching. His green eyes opaque with sated desire, Blair traced the contours of her mouth with his lips.

She pulled her head back to look deeply into her eyes.

"I'll never be sorry this happened," Jan whispered fiercely. She had never known anything so surely in her life. No matter what the future held for them, she knew that she would never regret this day and the happiness she felt at this moment.

Chapter Four

Later, they sat in Jan's gleaming kitchen sipping from cups of fragrant herb tea. They munched on thick slices of bread spread with butter and topped with Danish Harvarti. The rich aroma of the tea and the pungent scent of the cheese filled the spacious kitchen. They were both voraciously hungry but they preferred the quickly prepared bread and cheese to a more formal meal.

They were completely relaxed together but conscious of each other every minute. Blair was wearing only his gray jogging pants and Jan was wrapped in her cranberry housecoat. Her niggling fear of Blair and of her own body had been replaced by a feeling of euphoria. She was amazed that she could feel so totally relaxed in his company, so completely "at home" with him sitting across from her in her kitchen. She was glad that he had stayed for the afternoon, glad that they could talk so easily about almost anything. And she was even more glad of the wonder of their bodies, sated only moments before, but still drawn to each other like powerful magnets.

"It's strange," Blair said to her. "Here we are, living only blocks from each other, both of us lawyers. If we hadn't met in the park, I wonder if we would have met some other way, some other time?"

"Um-hmm," she answered, taking another sip of her tea. "We would have met some way."

"You sound very sure of that. Do you think it was fate that brought us together?" he asked teasingly.

"Something like that," Jan answered seriously.

"That's funny. I thought it was your competitive spirit. A lawyer and a runner, too. Sometimes I wonder what I'm getting myself into."

Jan grinned as she said, "I'll bet you're thinking how much easier our relationship would be if I were a waitress or something like that."

"Exactly."

"Well, don't worry, I won't cramp your style, either running or lawyering. Let's both take a vow to keep our business and personal lives separate, right from the beginning. We shouldn't have any problems with our careers," she said seriously. "I want to practice domestic law and you want to practice corporate law, and those are two areas that couldn't be farther apart. So, I guess we're safe there."

Blair raised his eyebrows in that maddening gesture that was beginning to be so familiar to Jan.

"You mean you don't think it would be fun to battle it out in court? Where's your competitive spirit now?"

"Oh, don't worry, I haven't lost my spirit. I just think it would be hard to fight it out all day, then snuggle up together at night. I like to give one hundred percent of myself to my cases and I'm not sure I could do that if you were on the other side. I might be tempted to compromise and give less than my clients deserve, and I wouldn't want to do that."

"That sounds very noble."

"I guess it does," Jan said with a slightly embarrassed grimace.

But Blair was clearly quite interested in learning

her point of view. "You make it sound as if your clients are very important to you. But is it your clients you care so much about, or is it the law?"

"I care about the law and the protection of the innocent, but my individual clients are important to me, too," Jan answered.

"Let me ask you a hypothetical question, then."

"Go ahead."

"Say you're representing a man who wants custody of his minor child. Naturally, you're giving him the best possible representation. Then, in the middle of the trial, something comes to light that proves beyond the shadow of a doubt that the man is an unfit parent. What do you do then?"

"I would try to talk the man out of seeking custody."

"And if that didn't work?"

"Then I would simply remove myself as his counsel," Jan answered without hesitation.

"But then the man would just find someone else to represent him."

"Possibly. Even probably. But I wouldn't have the child's future on *my* conscience." For several minutes, Blair had been running his fingers lightly up and down Jan's arm, gently massaging the fingers of her hand. Now she withdrew her hand from his and placed it in her lap. Serious conversation required serious concentration, and she couldn't concentrate with him touching her, making a soft touch on her arm an intimate gesture. "I guess I don't have to ask how *you'd* handle the same hypothetical situation," she finally said.

"Stand behind your client and do everything within your power to give him the best possible legal representation. After all, it's not my job to decide whether he's guilty or innocent. That's my philosophy in a nutshell."

Blair was grinning from ear to ear, but Jan could sense that he was serious. The fact of a client's guilt seemed to mean next to nothing to him.

"You certainly didn't learn that in law school," she answered, somewhat surprised that their attitudes toward their professions differed so greatly.

"No, I learned that in the real world." Jan started to speak, but Blair silenced her with a wave of his hand. "What about the woman who wants to divorce her husband of twenty-odd years because she's sick of listening to him snore?" he asked. "Is she completely innocent? Do you ever ask her to bring her husband in for a conference so that you can determine which one of them is really the injured party?"

"Of course not," Jan replied. "We were talking about guilt or innocence, not injury. In a case like the one you're describing, *both* parties are probably innocent." Before she could say anything more, Blair had pushed back his chair and rounded the table to gather her into his arms.

"That's enough talk for today," he instructed. He covered her mouth with his and quite effectively prevented her from carrying their friendly disagreement any further.

"There is one more thing I want to talk about," Blair said when they were clearing the table and stacking the dishes in the sink. "What were you thinking when I didn't call Thursday?"

"I thought you were angry with me because I didn't let you come up after our date," Jan confessed.

"I would find it very difficult to be angry with you, my darling, and even more difficult to *stay* angry."

"But the way you just walked off—"

"It wasn't easy to be turned away at the door by the most sensual woman in New York," he teased. "But if I gave you the impression that I was anything other than simply and totally frustrated, I'm sorry."

He was standing right behind Jan, and when she turned from the sink, she stepped into his arms. His lips met hers and confirmed his apology, as Jan proved her forgiveness by returning his lingering kiss with tender passion.

"Your lips are like satin," he murmured as he ran his tongue across them. "Satin lined with velvet."

"When I was a little girl my mother told me I tasted like strawberries." Jan laughed.

"She was wrong. You taste like honey and exotic spices that I've never tried before. Honey and spices sprinkled on velvet."

"I love your eyes," she told him when the kiss finally ended. She lifted slender, delicate fingers to trace the smile lines at the corners of his eyes. "They change all the time," she said, amazed at how free she felt to tell him these things. "I can almost tell what you're thinking by watching your eyes." She fell silent then and closed her eyes.

"What are you thinking about?" he asked.

"Just that I wish I had met you twenty years ago. I wish we had grown up together. I've already missed so much of your life. There are so many things I'll never know about you."

She smiled sadly and Blair wiped a single tear from her smooth cheek.

"I'll tell you everything," he promised, "even the truth about the sixth grade."

"I'm serious, Blair," she said, halfway between laughter and tears.

"So am I." His lips grazed her arms, her shoulders, with light butterfly touches that left her trembling even in the aftermath of their recent lovemaking. "We'll grow old together," he continued, "and someday it will seem as though we've always been together, that there was no time before we met."

"Will it really be like that?" Her voice held wonder and a longing that would have touched the hardest heart.

"I swear it."

"Hold me," she begged, and he did, making her forget the past and the future and everything except this one perfect day in her life.

Blair finally left early in the evening, after they had dozed in each other's arms and made love one more time, gently and sweetly, with perhaps a little less raw passion but with much more tenderness.

Jan was somewhat relieved when Blair suggested that he leave. Both of them pleaded "things to do," and Jan supposed that Blair, too, needed a little time alone to sort out his thoughts and feelings. Things were happening so fast, it seemed unbelievable that she had met him just a few short days ago.

She intended to take a long, luxurious bubble bath, wash her hair, do her nails, and then spend the remainder of the evening thinking about Blair, a diversion that she anticipated with the same pleasure she now found in his company.

When he kissed her good-bye at the door, she almost changed her mind and implored him to stay. And when he was gone, she wandered through the empty apartment like a lost soul, longing for him to return. EMPTY. That was the word that seemed to jump out at her from every corner. Her lovely apart-

ment had never seemed so empty before and she
had never felt so alone.

When Blair had dressed to leave, Jan had thrown
on a pair of pink lounging pajamas to see him to
the door. Now, she wandered through the apartment like a shimmering pink ghost. Like a forlorn
puppy inspecting strange quarters, she poked into
every corner, looking for some lingering sign of her
lover. But he was gone, as though he had never
existed. Had he been merely a figment of her over-
worked imagination? No, she told herself firmly as
she rubbed her arms to bring warmth to her cooling
skin. No, you couldn't have imagined what happened to you today. And her heartbeat accelerated
remembering what she and Blair had experienced
together.

Still, Jan continued to wander aimlessly through
the familiar rooms, wondering how they could suddenly seem so alien to her.

The apartment was a visual expression of Jan's
eclectic taste. Her love of unusual color combina-
tions sang out in the lime and blue bedroom with
its matching bath. But she could only see the bed
where Blair had made love to her. Her culinary
skill was evident in the sparkling kitchen, which
was a gourmet cook's delight of hanging pots and
utensils and drawers filled to overflowing with unusual accessories. But nothing in the room seemed
as charming to Jan as the table where they had
shared bread and cheese and held hands like new-
lyweds.

She looked into the spare bedroom and felt even
more lost. There was no memory of Blair Wynter
there. It was the only room in the apartment that
retained the original flat white paint on the walls
and tweedy brown carpeting on the floor. It housed

Jan's desk, her files, her new IBM Selectric. At the door to that room, Miss Janelle Richmond was replaced by J. Richmond, Attorney at Law. Somehow, it hadn't seemed right to try to compromise that room, and now it seemed wrong to try and fill it with Blair's presence.

The living room with its adjacent dining area was Jan's favorite place in the apartment. There were plants everywhere, in every window, swaying in delicate baskets hung from the ceiling, resting in huge tubs on the floor. She had chosen a subtle golden beige for the walls, with brown-and-beige-striped French wallpaper for one dining-room wall. The dining table was glossy hard wood, and it was surrounded by six matching chairs with white leather seats and backs. Jan had ordered a custom-made couch in white leather, seven feet long, and two chocolate-brown chairs patterned with apricot-gold stripes. Her pièce de résistance was the gorgeous apricot carpeting that had cost her nearly a month's salary.

It was all worth it. But now Jan looked at her sumptuous retreat in a new light. She looked around her and saw rooms empty of the presence of Blair Wynter and she knew that they would always be just that. She had known Blair only a short time, but she knew how she felt about him. Wherever she went in the future, whatever she did, he would be as important to her as the walls that surrounded her, as necessary as the air she breathed. Without him, there would be only empty space and material things that meant next to nothing.

After looking around her one last time, Jan made her way back to the bedroom. She had promised herself a hot tub full of bubbles, a cup of steaming herb tea, then a restful night filled with pleasant dreams of Blair Wynter. And she kept her promise.

She was awakened from a deep sleep by an incessant ringing noise, which she groggily identified as the telephone.

"Hello?" Eyes filled with sleep, she couldn't quite make out the time on her bedside clock.

"Good morning. Did I wake you up?"

"Blair? What time is it?"

"Exactly 6:05 A.M. I wanted to be the first person in the whole world to wish you a good morning."

"Well, you certainly managed to do that."

"So, aren't you going to say good morning?"

"Good morning, Blair."

"Did you miss me?"

"I do now that I'm awake." Then she remembered the night before and the ache that had completely filled her heart and her body. "I missed you last night, too."

"Can I see you today?"

The sound of his voice was doing strange things to her. "What did you have in mind?" she teased, knowing exactly what he was thinking of.

"Oh, I don't know. We could just play it by ear. Lunch, a walk in the park, who knows?"

"Sounds interesting," she answered. "What time will you pick me up?"

"How does about six-twelve sound to you? I'm right around the corner from your place, squeezed into an airtight phone booth. I've been running since five. I'm tired and sweaty and hungry, and I really need to see you. It's a glorious morning, too beautiful to spend alone. Anyway, I *have* to see you, to prove to myself that you're not just a figment of my imagination."

"Oh, I'm real, I can assure you of that."

"I'd rather find out for myself. How about it?

"Hey, come on, you could at least offer me breakfast," he coaxed when Jan didn't answer.

Jan wanted to see him. There was no question in her mind about that. But yesterday was still too fresh in her mind. It had been far too special and too wonderful—even talking about it now might make it appear to have been ordinary. She needed time to savor yesterday's magic, time to wind down slowly from the breathtaking high of the day spent making love. And if she invited Blair to come up now, and if he wanted to make love again and she didn't, he might get angry. He might say something she didn't want to hear and sully the memory of their day together. It was just too soon to put herself into that kind of a situation.

All these thoughts ran through her mind in the split second before she made her decision and jokingly answered Blair's question. "You may as well know right now that I never cook breakfast before noon. If you want to eat with me this early, I'm afraid you'll have to buy."

"Okay, I get the point." He sounded angry because she wasn't willing to let him come up to the apartment, but a moment later the tone of his voice changed and Jan sighed with relief. She didn't want to sleep with him again so soon, but she didn't want to anger him either.

"You win," he said grudgingly, "I'll buy. Throw on some clothes and I'll meet you in front of your building in ten minutes."

"Make it twenty and you've got a deal."

"Twenty, not a minute longer. I'm hungry."

"You're always hungry." Jan laughed.

"You could have made me forget about food this

morning," he threw back at her, "but now you've lost your chance. Get dressed."

The phone went dead in her hand and Jan smiled as she replaced the receiver and jumped out of bed. Twenty minutes! She rushed to turn on the shower and let it run while she started going through her closet.

The breakfast was delicious and being with Blair felt like breathing pure air again. With him, she was in a constant state of nervous excitement, constantly smiling at him for no reason, hanging on his every word, trying to commit every precious line of his face and body to memory.

When they had finished eating, they walked in the park for hours and talked about their past and about what they had planned for the future. Around noon, they ended up back at Jan's apartment building.

"Blair," she said, "I apologize for not asking you to come up, but Sundays are bad for me. I brought a lot of work home from the office this weekend and I didn't make much headway on it yesterday."

"No problem," Blair answered easily. "I have some work to finish up myself. But I'm glad we spent the morning together."

"So am I."

"I'll call you tomorrow."

He gave her a quick peck on the cheek and took off running down the street. Jan was unable to pull her eyes away from the sight of his graceful form as it grew smaller and smaller in the distance. She watched until he was out of sight, then went in to face the mountain of office work that awaited her.

Chapter Five

The next morning Jan awoke to azure skies and high-flying cirrus clouds floating across the sky on a brisk wind. It was her favorite kind of day, and her mood matched the day's perfection. The weekend with Blair had been a page torn out of her most private fantasies and she hadn't wanted it to end, in spite of mental and physical exhaustion. But after leaving Blair at noon on Sunday, she had worked hard all day, then gone to bed early and slept like a baby. Now, this morning, she was refreshed and ready to start the week in high spirits.

Standing in front of her full-length mirror, she found herself admiring the body that Blair had desired so ardently. Thinking about Blair brought a smile to her lips, a warm, tingling sensation to her body, and a blush to her cheeks. The face that stared back at her from the glass was the picture of a satisfied, contented woman.

She dressed carefully in a chocolate-brown suit that she complimented with a silky peach-colored blouse. She brushed her brown hair and efficiently knotted it on the nape of her neck. *J. Richmond, Attorney at Law.* But, for some reason, the transformation didn't seem complete. This morning J. Richmond wore a flush on her cheeks and a shine in her eyes that betrayed her strictly-business exterior.

Jan had agreed to meet Carole Downing at the courthouse, but she left the apartment early so that she would have time to drop by the office on her way. She loaded her briefcase, checked on her messages, then walked down the hall and tapped on the door to Mark's spacious office. When he didn't answer, she cracked the door as quietly as possible. He was sitting at his desk, completely engrossed in a volume of Blackstone. Jan closed the door behind her and an expression of pained annoyance spread on Mark's thin, handsome face, but when he looked up and saw that it was Jan who was interrupting him, he closed the thick book with a bang.

"Janelle, you look glorious. Peach is definitely your color."

"Thank you, Mark." Jan flushed and fussed self-consciously with the neck of her blouse.

"Sit down, dear." Mark waved his hand to indicate the comfortable leather chair on her side of the huge mahogany desk.

"Thanks, Mark, but I'm running a little late. I just wanted to check in and see if you have any instructions or suggestions." Jan stole a quick glance at the neat, white-gold watch on her thin wrist and relaxed a little. She still had over a half-hour.

"The Downing pretrial? No, Janelle, this is your case, not mine. I'm sure you're aware of all the ramifications."

"Yes, I think I'm on top of it."

"Fine, fine." He was openly staring at her face and Jan felt more than a little uncomfortable under his close scrutiny. "You really look lovely this morning. You have a *glow* about you. Is there something you haven't told me?"

"No, of course not. Mark, I really do have to run now."

"Well, you wouldn't tell me anyway. Go ahead, then. And good luck with the case." He smiled warmly and Jan returned his smile before turning and bolting from the room.

At the courthouse, she had barely enough time to confer with Carole Downing before their case was called on the pretrial calendar. When the court clerk called her client's name, Jan stood up and indicated that she was there to represent Carole. He then called John Downing's name several times with no response, and the judge was beginning to show her annoyance at the delay. Then there was a commotion at the back of the room as John and his attorney entered. Jan didn't bother to turn around. It was usual for lawyers to come flying into the courtroom just in the nick of time to save their client's case from being thrown out of court.

"Are you making an appearance for the complainant, Counselor?" the judge asked sternly, fixing the newly arrived lawyer with a wintry glance.

"Yes, your Honor. And I wish to apologize for my tardiness. My alarm clock—"

"We quite understand, Counselor." The judge's voice carried a modicum of sarcasm, although her smile was pleasant. Still, it wasn't the judge's voice that captured Jan's attention. The deep voice of the lawyer who had just entered the courtroom was strangely, hauntingly familiar. She turned and looked Blair Wynter straight in the face, her blue eyes locked with his green eyes, and both of them almost gasped with surprise.

"Well, I'll be damned!" was Blair's unprofessional exclamation when he finally recovered his power of speech.

"Oh, no," Jan moaned. "I don't believe it."

"You can not possibly be J. Richmond, Esquire," Blair said in a stage whisper.

"I can and I am," Jan retorted.

The judge chose this moment to clear her throat rather loudly. When she had both attorneys' full attention, she spoke softly but firmly.

"May I remind counsel that I insist upon professional conduct in my courtroom?"

Both Jan and Blair nodded meekly and answered, "Yes, your Honor."

"Very well, if that is understood, you may proceed. Mr. Wynter?"

Blair's first act was to present a substitution of counsel, naming Stu Underwood and Blair Wynter as the new attorneys for John Downing. Jan realized that there must have been a disagreement of some sort between John and his former attorney, which had forced his attorney to step down and have Blair's firm take over at the last minute. That explained why she hadn't seen Blair's name on the petition as attorney of record.

As Blair presented information to the court on John's behalf, Jan was overcome by a deluge of conflicting emotions. She was proud of Blair for his clear, concise presentation of the facts, even more remarkable since he obviously was not familiar with the case. She was angry with him for taking a case that she felt had no merit, since she didn't believe that Carole Downing should have to forfeit the custody of her children. But most of all, she was impressed because Blair was exactly the kind of lawyer she would have expected him to be, and she was devastated by his nearness. Blair had a special charisma that projected to every corner of the room.

Heat seemed to radiate between him and Jan,

but Blair had donned a cloak of cold, unemotional professionalism that would have hinted to no one that he and Jan were lovers.

When she rose to present her client's side of the case, Jan only hoped that her trembling legs would hold her up and that her voice would not break and betray her troubled emotions. The way she felt about Blair, the way her body responded to him, she was extremely uncomfortable arguing a case against him. She felt as if she suddenly lacked the advantage of the cool, concise reasoning that had always been her stock in trade.

But somehow, she managed to walk past the table where Blair sat without reaching out to touch him. She was able to stare just over his head when she addressed a remark to him, instead of looking into his cool green eyes. She even managed to still the trembling in her arms and legs until only she was aware of it.

As the morning dragged on, several major issues of the case were clarified, lists of possible witnesses were exchanged, and a trial date was set for three weeks in the future. As the lawyers conferred hurriedly with their clients and jammed papers and folders back into their briefcases, the court clerk was already calling the next case on the judge's overflowing docket.

Jan walked out into the corridor with Carole in tow. The woman was badly shaken by Blair's reiteration of her ex-husband's accusations about her character and her inability to raise her children properly. She had, of course, read his petition for custody, but it was far more unnerving to hear the issues spoken aloud before the court. Jan spent a few moments reassuring her client, told her to call the office for another appointment so that they could discuss the case in more detail, then looked around for Blair. As Carole got on the elevator, Blair emerged from the courtroom deep in conversation with a very smug John Downing. Blair was giving John some instructions about the coming trial and John was nodding his dark head and smiling like a Cheshire cat.

Jan turned her back on the scene and pressed the DOWN button for the elevator.

"Oh, Jan, hold on a minute," Blair called out as he gave John one last word of advice.

Jan winced as she saw Blair pat the man's arm reassuringly, then shake hands with him.

"Hi," Blair said when he had finally disposed of his client.

"Hi, yourself," Jan managed.

She was following her usual pattern with Blair. In his presence, she was torn with conflicting emotions. She wished that he wasn't involved in a case that could be so important to her. But she also wished that the case was *not* so important to her. She quickly denied the unbidden thought that she would have to choose between the two of them, between Blair and the Downing case, which was just another way of saying her career.

"I thought you promised that you wouldn't cramp my style?" The corners of Blair's mouth were turned up in a smile but only when she saw that his pale-green eyes also reflected a lighthearted mood did she relax a little.

"Didn't a lady lawyer ever cramp your style before, Mr. Wynter?" she asked teasingly.

"Usually I've been able to convince them of my superiority."

"Well, there's always a first time."

The elevator doors opened, and as soon as they

were inside, Blair leaned toward her. "I've missed you," he said as his lips grazed her cheek, then gently touched her lips.

"Me, too," she admitted as the blood in her veins responded to his touch with a warming flow.

"See you tonight?" he asked hopefully.

"Call me," was all Jan had time to answer before the elevator doors opened to the lobby, revealing a horde of impatient people waiting for a lift to the floors above.

He nodded and hurried out of the building ahead of her, calling out to another lawyer as he ran.

She stood on the courthouse steps and watched him walk rapidly down the street, talking heatedly to the other attorney. When he turned a corner and vanished from her sight, she stepped to the curb and hailed a cab to take her back to her office.

Throughout the long afternoon, Jan's thoughts were never far from Blair Wynter. She kept closing her eyes and conjuring up his image: clear, yet mysterious green eyes, thick, sandy hair, a wonderfully masculine, yet graceful body. She felt betrayed by the fact that Blair had taken on John Downing's representation, and although the rational side of her nature argued that she was being unfair, her feelings grew stronger as the day wore on.

Since her admission to the bar, Jan had not met a colleague whom she had thought of romantically. For some reason, other lawyers had never appealed to her, although some of them were very attractive men. But now, although she had only met Blair Wynter a few days ago, she knew that their relationship could be a serious one. The one thing that could come between them was Blair's involvement in a case that she was determined to win at all costs. She guessed that was why it seemed to be almost a personal betrayal that Blair had taken a case where he would be in direct competition with her, his experience and knowledge of the law pitted directly against hers.

Of course, Blair had said that he hadn't connected her with the J. Richmond listed as Carole's lawyer. But now that he knew, he certainly wasn't showing any sign of dropping out of the case.

After returning to her office, she interviewed a new client and had her secretary sit in on the conference to take notes, just in case her mind wandered. The client was a middle-aged man who wanted to buy an ice-cream-store franchise and make his fortune in thirty-six delectable flavors. The work was dull (a word Jan had never before associated with her work) and the man's excitement for his new venture barely made an impression on her. She totaled figures on her desktop calculator, made several recommendations, and finally advised the man that, as far as she could determine, the business was a sound investment. She then promised to have the bill of sale and other necessary papers drawn up by the following Monday, a statement that caused Barbra to sigh and look up from her note pad with a pained expression on her pretty face.

As Jan was shaking hands with the man and seeing him to the door, a buzzer rang on her desk, signaling that she had a telephone call waiting. She knew that it was Blair and she wasn't sure whether she was happy to hear from him or not.

"Jan Richmond," she announced into the phone's mouthpiece.

"I must have the wrong number. I thought this was the office of J. Richmond, Esquire." The thinly disguised voice was unmistakably his.

"You have the correct party," she answered coolly,

playing the game even as the receiver trembled in her hand.

"Well, don't melt the wires with your enthusiasm, sweetheart."

Jan leaned against a corner of her desk and motioned for Barbra to close the door on her way out.

Blair misinterpreted her silence and hurried on. "I got the message that you were a little upset about finding me in court representing John Downing this morning. I don't know how to convince you that I truly didn't connect you with the J. Richmond whose name appeared on the file. But I didn't. Okay?"

"Okay. That's not what I was upset about anyway," Jan answered, amazed that he had been able to read her so well. "Sooner or later, we were bound to wind up on opposite sides of a case, and I really couldn't expect you to call me up and warn me that we were going to meet in court. What worries me is your client and why you're representing him at all."

"I'll be glad to discuss that with you, Counselor. What do you say we do it over dinner?"

Jan would rather have continued the discussion over the phone. She knew it would be difficult, if not downright impossible, to discuss anything rationally while she was sitting close to Blair, staring into his eyes. "Fine," she answered, her need to be with him stronger at the moment than her need to win an argument. "Shall I meet you someplace?"

"How about the Berkshire? I'll meet you in the lounge around eight."

"Fine," she repeated, wishing that she had a little more power to resist him. She didn't want to be in any man's power, not even his. It was important to her to hold her own in any relationship. If she started jumping every time a man requested her to do something, soon there would *be* no relationship.

"The Berkshire at eight," he confirmed.

Jan hung up and glanced quickly at her desk calendar. If she could get out of the office by five-thirty, she would have time to shower and change into the new black pantsuit that she had been saving for just such an occasion.

Why do you want to go to that much trouble when you're so irritated with the man? she asked herself. But she didn't bother to answer her own question. She didn't have to.

Jan stood and walked around the office, massaging the back of her neck to ease the tension in her shoulders. My God, I hardly know the man and I'm already nervous as a cat about how I'm going to explain my most private thoughts and feelings to him. And even more nervous about how he's going to respond. Sometimes I wish I weren't quite so serious about the law. But that's how I am, and I don't really want to change. I want to believe in a person's innocence. Am I really at fault for caring about the people I represent and not wanting clients like John Downing, not wanting Blair to have them either? I can only hope that Blair is equally serious about his career, and that he won't demand sacrifices of me that I won't be able to make.

Somehow, she managed to get through the rest of the afternoon and out of the office by five-thirty.

Blair was waiting for her in the lounge when she arrived at the Berkshire Hotel at ten minutes past eight. As usual, he looked fabulous in a navy suit with a pale-blue shirt and a cranberry tie. His casual touch started blood rushing through Jan's veins, and need throbbing through her body. They sat in comfortable chairs with a glass-topped table between them, in a private spot near the back of the lounge.

Jan ordered a kir and Blair said he would have the same; then he settled back to appraise Jan's face and figure as several other men had done as she walked through the busy lobby on her way to the lounge.

"You look gorgeous in black," he said, letting his admiring gaze sweep up and down her trim figure.

"Why do men always feel obligated to comment on a woman's looks?" Jan asked, more annoyed at herself than at Blair. After all, she was the one who had chosen the sexy black suit, knowing full well what it did for her figure. "Why can't you simply say, 'I'm happy to be with you,' or 'It's nice to see you,' rather than try to build up my ego by telling me that I'm gorgeous?"

"All right." Blair leaned forward and reached for her hand across the low table that separated them. "It's nice to see you again and I'm happy to be with you. As a matter of fact, I'm *more* than happy to be with you."

"Oh, God," Jan moaned, "why do you have to be so . . . so *literal.* I suppose you'd love it if I told you that *you* were gorgeous?"

"Well, I wouldn't get uptight about it."

"You're impossible."

"So I've been told. Impossible and gorgeous." A grin spread across his handsome face, crinkling up the corners of his eyes and sending small tremors of longing down Jan's spine.

"I'm sorry," she said, returning the pressure of his hand. "I'm not angry, just annoyed with myself."

Their waitress arrived at that moment with long-stemmed glasses of chablis laced with crème de cassis, then discreetly left them alone again.

"To us," Blair toasted, clinking his glass lightly against Jan's.

"To us," she echoed.

"Now," Blair said decisively, after sipping the wine and returning his glass to the table. "Would you mind telling me why you were angry this morning?"

"I wasn't angry. I was . . . disappointed."

"With me, I presume?"

"Why don't we just drop it, Blair?"

"Remember that discussion we had about making a vow to keep our personal lives and our careers separated? Well, I don't think we're going to be able to do that. One of them is always going to overlap onto the other. So we might as well talk about it now."

"All right," Jan answered, setting her glass down on the table and meeting Blair eye to eye. "I wish you weren't representing John Downing. I wish we could have discussed it first."

"Listen, Jan, Stu Underwood accepted John's case over the weekend. He called me to tell me about it late Sunday night, then threw the file at me when I went in this morning. I hardly had time to glance at it before the hearing. Anyway, whatever your personal opinion of John Downing may be, the man is entitled to legal representation. Even the worst criminals are entitled to legal counsel."

"All right, I'll concede that point. Everyone is entitled to legal representation. But does that mean that *you* have to represent them?"

"Someone does," Blair answered matter-of-factly.

"I *hate* criminals and I don't particularly like men like John Downing," Jan said vehemently.

"Then you should have been a cop or a warden, not a lawyer," Blair answered, grinning broadly. "I told you how I feel about things like that, and anyway, John Downing is a long way from being a criminal by any stretch of the imagination. The man came to Stu asking for help, and Stu felt that we have an obligation to give him that help. And I might add that, as long as I'm working for Stu Underwood, I don't have a hell of a lot to say about it."

"I can understand that, but John Downing is a terrible person, Blair. I don't suppose he told you what he's done to his wife, how he tried to stifle her bid for independence and ruin her career. And that was just for openers, before he decided to try and take her children away from her. You can't possibly admire a man like that."

"I didn't say that I admired him, just that I'm representing him. Anyway, that's your client's side of it. The way John tells it, it's a completely different story."

"I'll bet it is, Blair," Jan said, leaning forward in her chair, "I'm sorry if I appear to be unreasonable. I just can't help but think that things like this are going to come between us."

"Only if we let them. And sweeping them under the rug isn't the answer."

"I know that."

"Jan . . ." Blair pulled his chair around the table, closer to hers, and draped his arm around her shoulders, which Jan thought was taking an unfair advantage. His hand rested on her right shoulder and burned through her jacket and her white silk blouse, warming the skin beneath. "I think we're going at this the right way and I'm all for discussing our feelings and our attitudes. But I don't think we should discuss the Downing case in particular. I don't think we should talk about it at all, if it's going to come between us."

"You're the one who insisted on discussing it," Jan reminded him.

"Oh, Jan, I wish we could quit being lawyers, just for one night. Let's pretend that you're a waitress and that I'm a truck driver. You can tell me how much you made in tips today and I'll see what I can remember about air brakes."

"The customers were all rude today," Jan played along, "and the tips were lousy. How was your day?"

"My brakes gave out and I think I ran over a dog. A terrible day. But you can make me forget it."

They laughed together and Jan's arms ached to reach out for him across the small space that separated them. She wanted to touch him, to feel his warmth, to slip her hands inside his jacket and feel the hard muscles of his back beneath her fingers. She wished that they could really forget what they were, for just this one evening. But she knew that it wasn't possible, because they were both the sum of all their years.

"Another drink?" he asked, his eyes and his hands continuing to work their magic on her.

"No, thanks." As they stood to leave for the restaurant and dinner, Blair's hand left her shoulder to grasp her elbow. His arm pressed against her side and warmth spread through Jan's body like a forest fire raging out of control. Suddenly she knew for a certainty that if she wanted to continue to be her own person, she would have to stay away from Blair Wynter, at least until she had time to sort out her feelings and establish her priorities. Her body's response to him was making it hard for her to look at their relationship objectively. A part of her, an *important* part of her, wanted nothing more than to give in and subjugate her hopes and desires to his, to follow blindly wherever he might lead her. But right or wrong, she had struggled for a long time to become the person she was today. And she could not commit herself to any relationship without a clear understanding of where it was going and what sacrifices would be required of her.

Chapter Six

The restaurant was elegant, the curried lamb superb, the clear white wine perfect. Only Jan's disposition was out of kilter. Her mood was one of quiet despair, because she knew that her relationship with Blair could not continue. She had to give herself some breathing space, some room to lay the foundations of her future as a lawyer. She had worked hard to graduate from law school with honors, land a job with a prestigious firm, and work herself up to a junior partnership. Now, she suddenly felt threatened and she felt that any major decision about her future as an attorney would have to be made without Blair's influence. She had to win the Downing case and, to do that, she had to be sure she could retain her objectivity. With Blair around, that could only become harder and harder to do. She was terribly afraid that his attitude about representing a client like John Downing and the way he felt about the law, in general, might influence her to do less than her best on the most important case she had ever handled. She could certainly not afford to dissipate her energies, splitting them between Blair and her career. Not now.

Blair's close proximity only made her feel worse, and she wished that she had not agreed to have dinner with him tonight. It would have been so much better if she had parted with him earlier, so much easier if she had not started to get used to him. Now she was beginning to become familiar with his ways and it would not be easy to tell him good-bye. Although she would not have missed making love to Blair for anything in the world, she was almost sorry that it had happened. Her heart felt as if it was being torn in two by the very thought of leaving him. For the first time in her life, she knew what people meant when they said they had a heartache. Now she knew that a heartache was a physical thing, a pain in your chest that was almost unbearable.

Even arguing with Blair was preferable to spending time in the company of any other man she had ever known. If only her career didn't mean so much to her . . . if only she hadn't worked so long and so hard to get where she was today . . . But she knew, deep in her heart, that there was no escaping it. A choice had to be made. She could only hope against hope that it wouldn't have to be a permanent choice, that sometime in the future she and Blair would be able to continue their relationship. But she couldn't count on that. The future was anything but clear, and she had to stop seeing Blair *now*.

The spicy, delicious lamb stuck in her throat as she thought of telling him, of turning him away.

After dinner, she refused Blair's offer of another drink and asked him to take her home.

It was still early when they returned to her apartment. She opened the door with the key, and blocking the door, she turned to face him. "Good night, Blair."

"That sounds more like 'good-bye' than 'good night,' but I'm going to give you some time to think it over. You've been moody all evening and I don't want you to say anything you don't really mean. I'll call you tomorrow."

Jan shook her head and hoped that he wouldn't notice the hot tears beginning to form in her blue eyes. "That's not a good idea," she managed to say in a thin voice that only vaguely resembled her own.

"Why not?" He didn't raise his eyebrows. Instead, he drew them together in a gesture that all too clearly asked Jan why she was doing whatever in the hell she was doing.

"This isn't going to work, Blair. I'm sorry."

His next words showed he was angry, not hurt, and Jan sighed with relief. She knew how to deal with his anger—his pain would have broken her heart.

"Do you know what your problem is, Jan?" he asked.

"No, but I'm sure you're about to enlighten me."

"You're damned right I am. It's about time somebody did." He was glowering at her, his green eyes dark with anger. "You're a spoiled brat who's never had to grow up. I knew another girl like you once—I knew her in the first grade. If she couldn't have her way, she refused to play."

"If that's what you think, you're not very perceptive."

"Then why don't you try to explain your problem to me."

Jan stood with her back to the apartment door and Blair leaned over her menacingly, his hands planted solidly on her thin shoulders. Jan ran hot and cold, her feelings for Blair burning like a fever, fighting for control over the icy detachment of her mind.

"John Downing—" she began, but Blair didn't want to hear it.

"Oh, my God! Not that again. Is that the only case you're handling?" he asked sarcastically.

"Of course not."

"Well, it's the only one you ever mention, and I think that's strange, since it's not even a very important case."

Jan's eyes flashed danger signals as she answered him icily. "It's important to me."

"I understand that. I just don't understand *why*."

"Blair, can't you see that it isn't the Downing case per se that's coming between us? I was simply using it as an example of the unbridgeable chasm between us. What's really tearing us apart are our beliefs, our basic—"

"No, you're wrong about that." Blair cut her off angrily. "What's coming between us is nothing more or less than your damned irrational need to win every game you play. If you hadn't beat me running the day we met, you probably wouldn't have spoken to me. Now you want me to stop representing John Downing so that I won't be competing against you in court. You always have to have the edge and, lady, let me tell you that I'm beginning to resent that."

"You couldn't be more wrong, Blair," Jan tried to explain. "I've never run from opposition and I never will."

"Maybe not—*if* you can choose your opponent and dictate the way he plays the game."

"Now wait just a minute—" Jan began, but Blair interrupted her again.

"That's another one of your stale lines. Maybe you need a new script writer."

"And maybe *you* need a new lover," Jan shot back.

"Maybe I do." Blair didn't bother with the elevator, but slammed through the service door that led to the stairs.

Jan entered her apartment on trembling legs, hung her coat up and let her suddenly weary body drop to the couch. A deep sigh escaped her as she curled up on the long white sofa and rested her aching head on one of its wide arms. She knew that she would never forget the look on Blair's face or the sound of his voice agreeing that everything was finished between them. At that moment, she had wondered if she was making a big mistake, over-dramatizing the conflicts in their relationship. Things certainly hadn't worked out the way she intended them to, with Blair storming down the stairs that way. She had wanted, above all else, to retain his friendship, to leave an opening for the future, once she had worked out her career moves.

But it was only too obvious that she would never see Blair Wynter again outside of the courtroom. Not if he had anything to say about it.

She remained on the couch in the dark living room for several long, sleepless hours. Blair's face swam before her eyes and her mind feigned relief while her heart was torn with regret. It was almost morning when she made her way to the bedroom and the questionable comfort of her lonely bed.

The next morning at work, Mark knew immediately that something was wrong, and before Jan knew what she was doing, she found herself sinking into the big leather chair in front of his desk, telling him about Blair.

"Janelle, darling, are you sure you're doing the right thing? Not that I question your judgment for a minute, but you *do* seem to care for the man. Maybe your career isn't quite as important as you think—"

A disbelieving Jan pulled herself together and cut him off. "I never thought I'd hear you make a remark like that, Mark. You've always encouraged me in my career, praised me for my independence and assertiveness."

"And I still do," Mark said, "so don't go jumping to premature conclusions. I simply intended to point out that perhaps you have come to a point in your life where you should start giving more attention to your personal life."

"At the expense of everything I believe in?"

"My dear Janelle, you always did have a flair for the dramatic."

"I'm not dramatizing, damn it, Mark. Was I wrong to think that I could count on you for a little sympathy?" Her dark-blue eyes were shiny with tears. At that moment, she didn't look a bit like a successful lawyer. Instead, she looked like a little girl, a terribly hurt and disappointed child who needed someone to hold her hand and tell her that everything would be all right.

"Oh, Janelle, you surely know that you can count on me for *anything*, at any time you need it." Mark leaned over her chair and tenderly wiped at her streaming eyes with his handkerchief. "Even if I hadn't promised your father that I'd look after you, you must know that I love you. You're the daughter that I never had, and never will now."

"Oh, Mark, I'm sorry. Now I've hurt you."

"No, no, darling, I'm fine. And you will be, too. But we must devise a plan to take your mind off Blair Wynter for a while. Then we'll talk again, when you've gained a better perspective."

"A plan?" Jan asked, slightly bewildered by Mark's entire attitude. She had assumed that he would be glad to help her wash Blair Wynter out of her life, with very little sympathy for her emotions. But he wasn't doing that. He was acting as if he thought she was making a mistake by not following the instincts of her heart.

"Yes," Mark continued, "a plan. And I think the first step will be for you to accompany me to the theater on Friday."

"Oh, I don't think so, Mark," Jan answered, trying to formulate an excuse. Somehow she just knew that she wouldn't feel any better or miss Blair any less by Friday.

"I'll pick you up at seven sharp," Mark went on, ignoring her protests. "Try to get out of the office a little early. We'll have to wait and grab a bite after the play, so munch on something while you're dressing."

There were times when Jan almost resented Mark's way of treating her as though she was a small child, but today she was eager to have someone take over and tell her what to do. If you want someone to tell you how to run your life, why not Blair? she asked. But as was usually the case when her alter ego asked her questions, Jan had no answer to that one.

It wasn't an easy week to get through. She worked on the ice-cream-parlor franchise, interviewed a man who didn't really want the divorce he was filing against his unfaithful wife, and set up a corporation to be used as a tax shelter by a clever small-business owner.

The only thing that gave her a real sense of accomplishment was the work she did on Carole

Downing's case. Still, she couldn't help but wonder if this sense of satisfaction would be enough to sustain her through all the long, lonely nights without Blair. There were moments (more than she cared to count) when she thought perhaps Mark was right, her career couldn't be that important. Her mind told her that her work counted most, but her heart kept intruding and trying to tell her that what she felt for Blair counted more.

By Friday morning, Jan had gotten to the point in her trial preparation where it was necessary to talk to Blair about the interrogatories they were going to take from some of the witnesses who couldn't appear in court. She wished she could just do without them, but it wouldn't have been either professional or practical to ignore something as important as the written questions she was allowed to ask witnesses before the trial began. So it was absolutely necessary to call Blair and find out how much liberty he would allow her in the range of questions she could ask.

She dialed the number, asked for Blair's extention, and waited anxiously for him to answer. When he finally did, it took every ounce of her strength to talk to him without blurting out an apology and begging to see him again.

"It's Jan Richmond, Blair," she announced, her voice catching on his name.

"Oh, hi, Jan." If he felt any emotion at the sound of her voice, Jan could not detect it. Face it, she told herself, you mean less than nothing to him now. Maybe you never did mean anything to him.

"I wanted to talk to you about the Downing case," Jan went on quickly, trying to keep her tone businesslike.

"So I presumed."

"Specifically, the interrogatories. I'm just getting ready to prepare them and I thought I should check with you first and maybe stipulate—"

"Ask anything you like, within reason," Blair cut her off. "If there's anything we object to, I'll give you a call."

"Okay, fair enough." She felt hurt that he didn't even seem to want to drag out the conversation. He was trying his best to get rid of her quickly and painlessly.

"Anything else?" he asked.

"No, I guess that about covers it."

"Okay, Jan. Nice talking to you."

"Yes, same here," Jan mumbled, close to very unprofessional tears.

He might as well have said "See you around," she mumbled angrily to herself when she had slammed the receiver down. The absolute nerve of that arrogant, self-centered . . .

But her anger ran down, to be replaced by the pain that hovered right behind it. Oh, Blair . . . Hot tears ran down her face and dropped onto her green desk blotter as she was confronted with the memories that the sound of his voice had brought back to her full force.

To be totally honest with herself, Jan had to admit that she was already beginning to regret her impulsiveness and have second thoughts about her decision to break up with Blair. But it was too late. She had made her bed, as the old expression went, and now she would have to lie in it.

Minutes later, Jan dried her eyes and pulled her spare makeup kit from the bottom drawer of her desk. She was grateful that her secretary hadn't popped in on her while she was shedding that river of tears. But the crying jag had done her some good.

It had washed away her anger and some of her pain, at least momentarily. It might have left her drained and headachy, but at least she was free of the crushing weight of her feelings for Blair Wynter.

In the afternoon, Mark reminded her of their "date" for the theater, then saw to it that she got out of the office before five o'clock. At home, she wearily climbed into a hot shower, hoping to be rejuvenated. Since morning, she had felt empty, a shell of the former Jan Richmond, lover of Blair Wynter.

She spent a long time on her makeup and hair, then dressed carefully in a teal-blue wool dress that was the exact color of her eyes. She started to put her long brown hair up in a twist, then decided to let it fall over her shoulders the way Mark liked it. The way Blair liked it.

Since it was going to be a chilly evening, Jan took her good winter coat from the dry cleaner's storage bag and threw it over her shoulders. It was a long black wool with a wide mink collar, her last winter's one expensive indulgence. She was pleased with her last-minute appraisal of herself in the full-length mirror and found that she was actually beginning to look forward to the evening in Mark's company. At least, with Mark she could be herself and not have to worry about displeasing him. It was nice to know she would be loved and appreciated with no hassles to look forward to at the end of the evening.

She waited in the lobby of her building and at precisely seven o'clock a taxicab pulled up in front and she recognized Mark's silvery-gray head emerging from the back seat. She ran out and joined him before he had time to get out of the cab, wondering how he always managed to be exactly on time, even

when he entrusted himself and his flawless schedule to cabs and other public conveyances.

The seats Mark had obtained were the best in the
theater, and soon after the curtain went up, Jan
was able to forget her problems and lose herself in
the make-believe world on the stage. The first act
of the musical was marvelous, and Jan fully appreciated what she would have missed by staying home
to sulk instead of accompanying Mark to see the
critically acclaimed play. At the intermission, Jan
and Mark went out to the lobby. Mark ordered a
glass of wine from the bar, but Jan preferred a
quick sip of thirst-quenching water from the foun-
tain. They milled around in the babbling crowd,
nodding and smiling to several familiar faces. After
ten minutes or so, when Mark had just mentioned
that they should be getting back to their seats, Jan
spotted Blair several feet away from her.

"Oh, my God," she breathed, grabbing Mark's
arm. "It's him."

"Him?" Mark asked, following the direction of
Jan's tortured gaze. "Oh, *him*. Well, let's make it a
point to say 'hello.' You mustn't let him think you're
sitting home sulking, you know."

"Oh, no, Mark. I don't want to talk to him."

"Of course you do," Mark said, leading her through
the rapidly thinning crowd until they were standing beside Blair and his date.

"Good evening, Blair," Mark said with a little too
much camaraderie. "Enjoying the play?"

"Mark. Good to see you. Jan." Just the sound of
her name on his lips brought such a stab of memory
that Jan found herself looking at Blair through a
mist of unshed tears. He hesitated a minute before
he turned to the stunning redhead on his arm. "I'd

like you to meet Sara Underwood. Sara, Mark
Whitmann and Jan Richmond."

Jan wished she hadn't noticed the girl's full red
lips or the wide blue eyes that gazed adoringly at
Blair as he spoke. She did her best to be gracious
for the two or three minutes she was compelled to
stand there chatting. She was, at least, grateful
that no one offered to shake hands with her, since
her hands were as cold as ice and shaking like
leaves in a high wind. Her legs were trembling, too,
and she was glad when the house lights dimmed for
the second act, requiring them to return to their
respective seats.

Mark could see that she was upset and he did his
best to calm her. "Janelle, the girl couldn't be a day
over eighteen. You don't suppose—"

"Didn't you see the way she looked at him?" Jan
turned her sad, blue eyes on Mark. "Please don't
try to convince me that she's his cousin or something."

"I think you're overreacting again. Blair was obviously very pleased to see you. He—"

"Oh, please just forget it, Mark," Jan managed to
say before they were both forced to silence by the
resumption of the play.

Mark had reservations at Sardi's, so there was no
way Jan could beg off and go home, which was
what she really wanted to do. Glancing quickly
around the restaurant, she was grateful that Blair
and his date had obviously chosen some other loca-
tion for their after-theater meal, if food was what
they intended to share to finish off their evening.

The maitre d' greeted them and showed them to a
small table in a corner of the busy room.

"You look especially lovely tonight, Janelle," Mark
told her after he had ordered two glasses of chablis,

the only alcoholic beverage that he ever indulged in.

"Thank you, Mark. I wish I felt lovely."

"Still thinking about Blair Wynter?"

"I can't help it, Mark."

"Well, Janelle, you're a very intelligent girl, so I shouldn't have to tell you that you can't keep this up. It's not good for you. It's affecting your work at the office and ruining what was once your lovely disposition. You'll either have to put the man out of your mind or—" Mark made a dramatic pause and took an appreciative sip of his chilled wine.

"Or?" Jan prompted.

"Or go after him. Get him back. Oh, don't look at me like that. This is the nineteen-eighties and you're one of the most liberated young women I know. Why should it shock you to be told that you should go after a man if you want him?"

"The words don't shock me, just the fact that they're coming out of your mouth."

"I know, I'm not running true to form with my advice these days. But it's for your own good, Janelle. Since Bette died, I've learned firsthand how terrible it is to be alone. I don't want you to have the misfortune to grow old alone, my dear."

"Mark," Jan said, "don't ever try to write fiction. You're a lousy storyteller."

Jan knew that, although he missed his wife and had loved her deeply, he was thoroughly enjoying his bachelorhood.

"I resent the implications of that remark," Mark replied huffily. But he squeezed her hand and silently toasted her with his raised glass.

They ordered filet mignon with a tossed salad, since that was what Jan almost always had when she was dining with Mark. Sophisticated as he was in other areas, Mark was not curious about experimenting with food or drink. He ate mostly steaks and salads and drank only a dry white wine before a meal, water to accompany it, and a strong tea afterward. He was so set in his ways that Jan could readily understand why he didn't try to remarry after Bette's death.

After dinner, Mark took her home in a cab and saw her to her door.

"Think over what I said earlier, Janelle," was all he said before he disappeared. He could have saved himself the effort of reminding her, because that was all Jan had been thinking about during supper and the drive back to her apartment.

Since the moment she had seen Blair in the theater lobby, her limbs had been trembling uncontrollably, and she had felt close to the brink of tears. A pulse beat at the very center of her body, and the blood pumped through her veins in a steady tattoo of desire. There was no denying that she wanted Blair, or that she needed him. Her body needed him for its fulfillment and another more secret part of her needed him just as badly. She felt as if he had already become a part of her, a part that couldn't be cut away without great loss. The ache deep in her chest proclaimed to her that she couldn't live without Blair Wynter, and as corny as that sounded, she knew it was true. Without Blair, her heart would slowly stop pounding, her body would shrivel and die. Without him, she was less than nothing.

Nothing had really changed in the week since she had broken up with Blair. Nothing except her knowledge of her own limitations. She had been so worried about sacrifice, but only now did she know what sacrifice was. If there was any way at all to make their relationship work, Jan knew now that she would have to find it. If they disagreed on how their careers should be handled, then they would have to work harder at keeping their careers separate from their private lives. For once, Jan needed another human being more than she needed to know that she was right.

But she still hated to admit that some of Blair's accusations had hit home. He had accused her of being afraid to compete with him professionally. But he didn't understand that she wasn't afraid of losing to him. That thought had never crossed her mind. She was only afraid of what the competition would do to their relationship.

Jan undressed, hung up her clothes, and prepared for bed with the memory of Blair's face and body hovering before her eyes. The only bright spot in her life was the fact that she knew she would dream about him tonight. Even J. Richmond, Esq., would not be able to interfere with her dreams.

Chapter Seven

❧

The light of day was just beginning to touch Jan's windows when she jumped out of bed as though she had been shot out of a cannon. She was halfway across the room before she came fully awake and stopped her headlong rush to nowhere.

She turned and looked back at her bed. It was a tangle of white blankets and lime-green sheets. Her pillows were both on the floor several feet from the bed, where she must have thrown them. Whatever I was dreaming about, she mused, it must have been interesting.

A glance in the mirror over the blue vanity in her bathroom confirmed that Jan's person was as disarrayed as her bed. Her long hair was a tangled mass and her creamy silk nightgown showed a small tear in the lace at the low neckline.

She fingered the soft Belgian lace, sick at heart over the tiny rent in the delicate fabric. She could recall vividly the Saturday morning last spring when some impulse had made her lay aside the practical pajamas she had chosen and, almost giddily, purchase the gorgeous eggshell gown instead. She hadn't worn it before last night, when she had lifted the silky gown from its nest of white tissue and slipped it over her slim shoulders in a futile effort at repairing her damaged ego. She had needed to feel as feminine as possible after seeing Blair in the company of the beautiful young redhead. Now she was sorry she had worn it, because she would have to have it repaired before she could wear it again. But what does it matter? she asked herself glumly. Who am I saving it for?

Jan could remember nothing of the dreams that had haunted her restless sleep, except the smiling face of the girl on Blair's arm in the theater. That lovely face had seemed to float before her in the night, taunting her.

Her body ached fiercely. She felt as though she had been used as a punching bag during the long, terrible night. She was tired and sore and had no desire to leave her apartment. She forced herself to dress in old jeans, shop for groceries, straighten the apartment, then take in a solitary movie to break up the long, boring weekend.

On Monday morning she was up early, dressed for work in a trim beige suit with a chocolate blouse and matching accessories. She pulled her hair back in a tight twist, almost daring herself to look good. Well, J. Richmond, if you end up as an old maid, remember that you asked for it, she told her frowning mirrored image.

By the time she got to the office, after spending almost forty minutes bogged down in a morass of slow-moving vehicles with a grumpy cabby, she had made a decision. Or, rather, she had rethought her previous decision and concluded that she had been a terrible fool, hurting no one but herself with her self-righteous attitude.

She walked straight to her office and closed the door tightly, a sign to Barbra that she didn't wish to be disturbed. She removed her coat, hung it up, and threw her unopened briefcase on her desk. Then, supporting herself against the desk, she dialed Blair Wynter's number with trembling fingers.

"Mr. Underwood's office," the receptionist answered with a smooth British accent.

"Mr. Wynter, please," Jan said, trying unsuccessfully to control the tremor in her voice.

"Mr. Wynter is on another line. May I ask who's calling?"

"Never mind, I'll call back." Jan replaced the receiver quickly, almost guiltily, hoping that the girl hadn't recognized her voice from her previous calls. She didn't want anyone warning Blair that she would be calling back, just in case he wanted to avoid her.

Deciding that she would try again in ten minutes, Jan buzzed her secretary and asked if there were any calls. There was only one. Someone had called while she was on the other line, but he hadn't left a name or a message. Jan wasted the next few minutes sharpening pencils, aligning and straightening the files on her desk, and doodling Blair's name on a fresh yellow legal pad.

Exactly ten minutes after her first call, she dialed Blair's number again, only to find that he was still talking on the other line.

Five minutes later, she tried a third time.

"Mr. Wynter is still tied up. Would you care to leave your name and number?"

Jan felt like just hanging up again, but she knew that would be silly. "Yes," she answered quickly. "Tell him Jan Richmond called. He has my number."

Her hand was still resting on the telephone when it rang, startling her.

"Hello," she answered shakily.

"Am I speaking to Jan Richmond or J. Richmond,

Esquire?" It was Blair, and the deep, rich tone of his voice was the most beautiful sound Jan had ever heard. She had to bite her tongue not to tell him so.

"It's Jan, Blair. And I need to talk to you, to explain."

"If you're apologizing, I accept. Now don't hang up, that was supposed to be a joke." His voice sunk to a low, husky whisper that floated into Jan's ear. "I love you, Jan Richmond, and I know you love me. That's all that matters. Everything else will work out. I promise you that."

"Oh, Blair, I'm so glad I swallowed my pride and called."

"*You* called? When?"

"Why, just a few minutes ago. I left a message. Aren't you returning my call?"

"Are you kidding? I've been trying to reach you all morning. First you weren't in, then you were on the phone. This is at least my fourth attempt."

Jan laughed and hugged the telephone receiver to her chest, wishing that she could reach out and hug Blair.

"I've been trying all morning, too," she told him. "What's that expression about great minds running in the same direction?"

They laughed together and agreed to meet for an early lunch. When she hung up, Jan began to count the minutes that passed far too slowly until they were together again.

She had gone halfway across the room when she suddenly realized what Blair had said: "I love you, Jan Richmond, and I know you love me." He had said that he loved her! Falling in love hadn't been included in Jan's carefully laid plans, but a man like Blair Wynter came along only once in a lifetime.

Thank God she was getting a second chance to accept his love. "He loves me," Jan said aloud, and felt like shouting it from the top of the building, for all the world to hear.

After that, there was no chance of getting any work done for the remainder of the morning. She sat in her desk chair and stared out her window at the blue sky that looked to be only an arm's length away, savoring Blair Wynter's words in her heart.

An hour later, she was sitting in a cab next to Blair, bound for his favorite park. Although food was not uppermost in either of their minds, they stopped off at a deli and had the cab wait while they ordered pungent hot pastrami on rye, which they carried in a brown paper bag to a bench in Bryant Park. It was a beautiful, sunny fall day, and only when the errant wind touched them did they remember that it was October.

Jan ate slowly, savoring the rich delicatessen food and the nearness of Blair Wynter, who had just hours ago seemed to be on the far side of an un-bridgeable gap. He was wearing a three-piece brown suit with a pale-yellow shirt that made his hair look almost blond in the sunlight, and she thought he was as handsome as any movie idol. She suddenly felt ravenously hungry, but was full before she had consumed a third of the huge sandwich. When the butterflies in her stomach continued to dance, she realized that he had made her stomach feel weak and empty, not the lack of food.

They strolled through the park holding hands, not the only young lovers to take advantage of the lovely weather. At a flower stand, they stopped to admire the colorful mums, bringing a smile to the face of the elderly woman who tended the blossoms. Then, at a book stall, Blair found an old, dog-eared copy of the poems of Elizabeth Barrett Browning. He bought it for Jan and, at her insistence, inscribed it with an artistic flourish: "For the most complete woman I have ever known. Welcome home."

Clasping the treasured book to her chest, Jan took a deep breath and asked the question that had been nagging her for the past hour: "I know it's none of my business, Blair, but who is she?"

"She?" he asked innocently, his green eyes dancing with mischief.

"The redhead," Jan answered, clearly exasperated.

"Oh, my sweet little Jan is jealous. I think this may just be worth all the misery you've put me through the past few days."

"Are you going to tell me who she is?" Jan didn't think he was the least bit funny.

"That lovely young lady happens to be my boss's niece, who was passing through the city on her way to New England. If you had been paying attention, you might have noticed that her last name is Underwood. Stu made plans to take her to the theater, then had to cancel out at the last minute. Since I had nothing better to do, I volunteered."

"You'd better be telling me the truth, Blair Wynter," Jan threatened.

"Scout's honor," Blair replied solemnly.

"She was so beautiful, and so young."

"Just nineteen. And gorgeous. But she wasn't Jan Richmond."

And that was all Jan needed to hear.

They had barely enough time to admire the lovely formal gardens before it was time to hail a cab and hurry back to their respective offices. As the cab careened around a corner, they leaned against each other and Blair's arm encircled Jan's waist to keep her from moving away again. He kissed her ten-

derly and whispered in her ear, to the delight of the
cabby, who was smiling at them in his rearview
mirror.

"I want to see you tonight. I *have* to see you
tonight."

"I'll be late getting out of the office. For some
reason, I seem to be getting behind on my work."

"How late?"

"Oh, maybe six-thirty or seven, if I'm lucky."

"Come straight to my place. I'll fix dinner, then
I'll walk you home later."

"*You'll* fix dinner?" Earlier Blair had confessed to
eating most of his meals in restaurants, since he
could hardly boil water without burning it.

"I'll have you know that I flip a pretty mean
flapjack."

"Pancakes for dinner?"

"It's either that or eggs, take your pick."

"Eggs would be fine," Jan answered, wondering
how much damage he could do to a simple egg.

"I'll be expecting you around seven." He kissed
her again as the cab pulled up in front of her
building, and she had to bite her tongue to keep
from confessing her love in front of the throngs of
hurrying New Yorkers on the sidewalks.

Throughout the remainder of the afternoon Jan's
mind kept returning to Blair's soft lips on hers in
the taxi, his hands firm and insistent, the little-boy
look on his face when he offered to make dinner for
her. She sat through a long, boring office conference where Mark discussed several important cases
that the firm was privileged to handle, cautioned
the younger members of the staff on proper dress
and decorum (no blue jeans, not even on Saturdays),
and threatened to stop buying paper clips altogether
if the secretaries didn't stop using thousands of

them weekly. Jan wondered briefly just how she could pass this information on to Barbra without sending her into gales of laughter, then her mind returned to Blair Wynter and stayed there for the rest of the conference.

On her way out of the conference room, she was stopped by Mark's hand on her shoulder. "You're smiling, Janelle. Does that mean that you and Mr. Wynter have settled your differences?"

"Does it show that much?" Jan blushed happily and looked instantly younger and prettier.

"It shows, and it looks lovely on you. Maybe my fatherly advice helped a little, then."

"Oh, it did, Mark. I've meant to say thank you."

"Never mind. You're happy, that's all that counts." He patted her arm affectionately and walked off down the hallway.

Jan hurried back to her own office. She had a lot of files to go over and tons of dictation to catch up on before she could leave for the day.

At six-thirty she stacked the last file in her OUT basket and left the dark, deserted offices of Babcock, Wynne & Whitmann.

Blair met her at the door to his apartment and kissed her firmly before taking her coat and briefcase.

"I hope you like Chinese," he said, leading her into the tiny alcove that served as a dining area.

"I love it, but you—"

"Just feast your eyes," he silenced her. The table was covered with a pale-blue cloth, set with bright-blue stoneware, decorated with yellow candles and varicolored mums. It was lovely, and it was spread with enough Chinese food to feed a small army. Blair lifted the lids of small Corning Ware dishes and displayed aromatic wonton soup, egg rolls, pepper steak, and fluffy white rice. There were also flat yellow bowls filled with Chinese noodles and mustard sauce.

"A real gourmet meal. I'm proud of you, darling." Jan pecked him on the cheek.

"There's more," Blair said proudly. He went to the kitchen for a steaming pot of Chinese tea and a dish of fortune cookies. When Jan followed to offer her help, she collapsed into helpless laughter. The kitchen sink was overflowing with square white boxes bearing the logo of Jan's favorite Chinese restaurant, which was just blocks from Blair's apartment.

"You cheated," Jan accused when she had finally stopped laughing.

"No, I didn't. If I'd wanted to cheat, I would have concealed the evidence."

"True. But why didn't you just throw a couple of eggs in a skillet?"

"I wanted to pamper you, to do something nice for you. It's good to have you back, Jan." He sat down on one of the high-backed chairs in front of the table and pulled her down onto his lap. "I want to make love to you. Right now."

"Not right now. I'm hungry." Jan weakly resisted his warm breath on her neck, his smooth hands pulling her chocolate blouse free of her beige skirt.

"We can eat later," Blair murmured, his hands on the smooth skin of her back raising goose bumps.

"Blair, we can't spend every minute we're together making love." Jan laughed as she tried to straighten her skirt and rearrange her blouse. "Besides, the food will get cold."

"To hell with the food," Blair growled against her throat. He ran rough hands up her warm, stockinged legs, and Jan sighed and settled on his lap again. She rested her head on his broad shoulder, feeling safe and secure from the storms of life. She felt that nothing bad could ever happen to her as long as she remained in the harbor of Blair's embrace.

"Oh God, it feels so good to have you back again," he said, mirroring her own thoughts. "My arms have ached to hold you this way."

She closed her eyes and relaxed her body against his, giving herself up to the joy of his touch. His hands were so warm, so strong as they stroked her arms and caressed her shoulders and gently cupped her breasts. She admitted how much she had missed him, how much pain she had been hiding from herself. Her chest rose and fell as he worked with the small pearl buttons of her silk blouse. Then her breasts were free and he bent his head to take them in his mouth. His tongue licked her nipples and they rose to taut peaks of exquisite sensitivity. Then he raised his head and carried the rich, spicy taste of her to her own mouth.

She breathed deeply and sucked at his tongue, his lips. Then she thrust her own tongue gently between his teeth and explored the satiny, hot lining of his mouth.

"Oh, Blair," she murmured as his hands moved to the zipper of her skirt.

"It's been so long," he whispered, biting on her earlobe and inflaming her mind and her body with sweet desire.

"Too long," she agreed as she reached to unbutton his shirt and help him out of it.

Both naked to the waist, they stood and fell against each other. Blair's hands moved up and down her spine in a slow, caressing motion and Jan heard herself begging him to make love to her.

"The food will get cold," he teased, pretending to push her away. "Aren't you the one who was starving a few minutes ago?"

"I am starving," she answered, clinging to him.

Releasing her, Blair walked to the couch and tossed its two small pillows to the floor. Then, as he kissed her deeply and hungrily, they sank slowly to the beige shag carpet and knelt facing each other, joined by their lips and their eyes. He thrust his tongue slowly in and out of her parted lips in a slow, rhythmic motion that maddened Jan until she grabbed his tongue with her teeth. She bit on his lower lip and he growled with something more than pain. Then Blair bent her over and arranged the pillows under her, one for her head and one for her hips.

"You're beautiful, Blair," Jan murmured dreamily as he stood over her removing his own clothes. He laughed and fell to his knees between her parted thighs.

"So are you, my love. I want to please you every way I know how."

"Show me," she urged, her voice thick with desire.

His sandy hair fell across her stomach as he bent his hungry mouth to her soft flesh. When he raised his head and leaned forward, Jan reached for him and guided him into her, then fell back across the pillows he had placed beneath her. His body crushed her to the floor and his first thrust was a shock of pain. But every movement after the first became sweeter and more pleasurable until Jan was bursting for release. Her blood pounded in her ears as she raised her body to meet his and wound her long legs around him to draw him back to her.

As Blair's breath became ragged, Jan closed her eyes and gave herself up to the sensations of raw pleasure that were coursing through her body. Together, they reached the summit of ecstasy, straining against each other, holding each other with a terrible possessiveness.

As he rested on top of her and struggled to get his breath, Blair's hands clutched both sides of her face and his green eyes drilled into hers.

"Don't ever leave me again, Jan," he ordered.

"I won't." She would have been afraid to refuse him.

"Promise me," he insisted, his breath hot on her cheek. "Tell me you'll never leave me again."

"I promise," she answered, then smiled, confident with the knowledge that his pain when they were separated had been as great as hers.

With the same intensity, Blair gently stroked her cheek and brushed his fingers across her lips. "I love you, Jan," he said with tenderness in his voice and in his eyes.

"I know you do." Jan smiled up at him and reached to wind her fingers in his sandy hair. "I love you, too."

He traced the lines of her naked body with a light, sensual touch. His hands ran from her shoulders to her rounded breasts, from her flat stomach to the curve of her hips and thighs.

"When we were apart, I used to close my eyes and remember every part of of your body," he said, watching her eyes as his hands moved caressingly. "It was like watching an old film that you'd seen a dozen times, something you'd committed to memory so that you'd never have to lose it. I kept telling myself that it couldn't possibly be over between us. I wouldn't believe that it was over."

"I felt the same way," Jan admitted as she traced the contours of his face with trembling fingers. "I'm just thankful we both felt that way. I can't imagine what it would be like to never see you again, to never love you again."

Blair stood up and pulled her to her feet. Then he gathered her in his arms and carried her across the hall to his tiny bedroom, where he proved his love once more before he reluctantly accompanied her back to the dining room.

He picked up her plate and began stacking it with food from the serving dishes.

"I'm not *that* hungry," Jan protested as the plate filled with food.

"Just be quiet and eat," he told her. "When I think you're too stuffed to make a run for it, I plan to tell you the story of my life."

But, before he began to talk about himself, Blair wanted to know everything about Jan's family and her childhood. They were on their second cup of after-dinner tea and seated on the couch in Blair's small living room when he finally got around to telling her something about himself.

"My mother and father were divorced when I was ten years old," he said. "It came as a complete shock to me and it really tore me up. For a while, I thought they had split to punish me for something I'd done. I used to lay awake nights trying to figure out what I could have done that deserved such awful punishment. I used to spend Saturdays with my dad. We'd go to a movie and have a hamburger afterward. I guess that was my dad's idea of what it took to make me happy. And it was fine, except that what I really wanted to do was just spend time with him. I could have seen a movie any day of the week, but I could see my dad only on Saturday.

"Then he got sick and died and I was so damned lonely that I didn't think I could stand it. My mom

remarried a couple of years later and her new husband tried his best to be my friend. As a matter of
fact, we became good friends and we still are. But
he's never been a father to me, and I guess I still
miss my dad, after all these years."

"You've missed out on a lot," Jan said tenderly.
"Even though my parents seemed to live in a world
of their own, my dad was always there when I
needed him. And now that I'm away from him, I
have Mark to take his place."

"But you're talking about leaving Mark's firm
and opening your own office," Blair reminded her.

"That won't hurt our relationship. When I break
my professional ties with Mark, we'll still be friends.
He means an awful lot to me."

"I know how much I've missed," Blair said reflec-
tively, "and I don't want the same thing to happen
to a son of mine. I want my kid to feel that he can
talk to me, that I'm good for advice and understanding, not just the car keys."

"Whatever you want for your own children, Blair,
you wouldn't expect to give up your career for them,
would you?"

"Are we back to the Downing case again?" Blair
asked, clearly irritated by the turn their conversation was taking.

"No, we're not," Jan answered easily, "we're still
talking about Blair Wynter. That was a hypothetical question."

"Then the answer is 'no,' I would not give up my
career for him. But I *would* cut down my hours, if
they were too long, so that I could spend more time
with him. I would want to be there whenever he
needed me. And I would work hard at establishing
a good, sound relationship with him."

"You keep referring to 'him.' What if your children turn out to be daughters instead of sons?"

"You wouldn't dare," Blair teased, wrestling her into his arms and pulling her close.

"I don't know how much I'd have to say about it," Jan answered lightly. Then she decided it was a good time to throw in a serious question or two. "What about me, Blair? Would you expect *me* to give up my career to stay home and bring up a child? Because I wouldn't do that."

"You've already answered your own question," Blair answered, not too happily. "If you really believe that you couldn't do it, I guess I couldn't ask you to do it. I told you we'd work things out, and I meant it."

"You sound terribly disappointed."

"Believe me, Jan, I never planned on marrying another lawyer. I'm the kind of a man who needs a home and a family. I can't deny that I'd like to have someone waiting at the door every night with a hot dinner and a little TLC."

"But?" Jan encouraged, hoping that he would say what she wanted to hear.

"But I fell in love with you," Blair answered with an almost wicked smile. "So I guess I'll just have to put up with your idiosyncrasies."

"Now you're calling my career an idiosyncrasy."

"Well, isn't it? Women should leave jobs like lawyering and doctoring to the stronger sex."

"My God, you're turning into a chauvinist right before my eyes."

"I'm not changing, just being honest."

"Well, go on," Jan urged. "Since I got you started, you may as well give me the full benefit of your homespun philosophy."

"All right," Blair said eagerly. "For openers, the

practice of law can be a dirty business, Jan. It amazes me that you haven't figured that out yet."

"I know what being a lawyer is all about, Blair. I've already had my share of rape and assault cases. I was even co-counsel for an accused murderer last year. Not by choice—I didn't get a chance to refuse. Mark thought it would be good experience for me, whether I liked it or not."

"You don't have any idea what I'm talking about." Blair shook his head incredulously. "Murderers and rapists aren't the ones who make you wish you'd never taken the bar exam. At least they need your representation, whether you think so or not, and occasionally they're even grateful for what you can do for them."

"Then just who are the monsters I should be on the lookout for?" Jan asked with a smile.

"Smile if you like, but you're far too naïve for a city girl."

"I am *not* naïve," Jan answered, feeling sure that naïveté was something a female lawyer in New York City could simply *not* afford.

"You're too trusting, Jan." Blair put his hands on her shoulders and pushed her away from him so that he could look into her eyes. He held her at arm's length and caressed her face with his eyes. "For example, as soon as we met, you began to trust me implicitly. You let me walk you home, let me see where you lived. You were eager to talk about your work. What if I had let you talk, then used some of the things you said against you?"

"You wouldn't do that."

"How did you know I wouldn't? And how do you know the next guy won't?"

"Because there won't be a next guy." Jan slid inside the barrier of his arms and buried her head on his chest. He ran his fingers through her silky hair, and when he spoke again, some of the harshness had left his voice.

"I'm tempted to believe you," he murmured into her hair.

"You can. But to get back to your sage advice, are you trying to tell me to watch out for my unscrupulous colleagues?"

"Lawyers, judges, clients—you expect too much of all of them. You're idealistic, and idealism has no place in the modern world."

"I don't believe that, and I never will," Jan answered. "There's absolutely nothing wrong with trusting people, *or* with being idealistic. When you stop having dreams, you may just as well pack it all in."

"I didn't think I could convince you. Just don't say I didn't try to warn you."

Blair got up to change the record on the stereo turntable, then went back to gather Jan in his arms. She snuggled against him, grateful for the night and the music and his strong arms to hold her. But even in the midst of such content, doubts began to nag her. It was a good feeling to know that Blair loved her so much and wanted to protect her. They had talked about marriage as naturally and as easily as if they had known each other for years, instead of days. But Jan had never wanted to be protected from the world, and she didn't think she wanted to start now. She would have to prove to Blair that she was a very independent woman who liked to stand on her own two feet. She also knew that she didn't want to give up the way she felt about people in general, even if Blair did think she was being naïve. She had always found it better to trust people and expect the best of them. She found that her psychology worked most of the time. When a person sensed that you trusted him, he usually managed to come through for you.

In her opinion, Blair was far too negative in his dealings with his clients and with other attorneys. It just wasn't good policy to expect the worst of people and then sit back and wait for it to happen. You couldn't go through life measuring out your trust in careful doses. Well, maybe she would be able to change that, by proving to Blair that her way was better. At least, she would give it one hell of a try!

She eased herself out of Blair's arms and, a few minutes later, out of his apartment.

Chapter Eight

Jan spent the next morning in court handling the calendar call for the office. She had a prepared list of six or seven cases that were to be scheduled for various members of the firm. It was a chore she found very time-consuming, but since she had to be there, she hoped against hope that Blair would be handling the job for his firm. That would, at least, make the morning interesting. Her spirits dropped when she saw Stu Underwood swagger into the courtroom and take a seat on the far side of the room.

She had several other errands in the vicinity of the courthouse and it was almost noon when she jumped into a cab to return to her office. She stopped at a deli on Wall Street to grab a tuna-salad sandwich and a chocolate milk shake, planning to have lunch at her desk.

"Ms. Richmond, I didn't think you'd make it back before twelve. You have a lot of phone calls." The receptionist set aside her nail enamel to hand Jan a stack of pink telephone message sheets.

"Thanks, Sue. I like that shade of nail polish."

"Thank you, Ms. Richmond." The girl returned with a warm, if somewhat surprised, smile.

Jan glanced at the messages on her way back to

her desk and her heart did a series of flipflops when she read the second sheet in the thick pile.

"Mr. Wynter—called at 9:00, 10:15, 11:05, 11:40. Will call back. No message."

Smiling at the way her heart responded to the sight of his name written on a piece of paper, Jan dropped her bulging briefcase on her desk and tried his number.

"Mr. Wynter is out to lunch," the receptionist informed her icily. "Will there be a message?"

"Yes," Jan answered. "Please tell him that Ms. Richmond returned his call."

She was disappointed that she had missed Blair's several calls. He had probably wanted to treat her to lunch. And here she was, with a gooey tuna sandwich and a warm milk shake. She ate at her desk, thumbing through the rest of her telephone messages between bites, making mental notes on the calls she would have to return. She noted a call from Judge Miller and also one from Carole Downing. Well, the judge will be out to lunch now, she mused. I'll have to try to get ahold of her later this afternoon.

She dialed Carole Downing's business number and, luckily, found Carole in. After exhanging pleasantries and listening intently for several minutes, Jan hung up and angrily punched out Blair's number. He was in and had just been getting ready to return Jan's call.

"Blair, let's take care of business first," Jan began. "I just talked to Carole Downing and it seems we have a small problem."

"Just what I need today, another problem." Blair sighed wearily, then said, "Okay, I guess you'd better tell me about it."

"Well, it seems that John and Lisa had the kids over the weekend, and according to Carole, they weren't very discreet about what they discussed in front of John and Missy."

"I guess that means they talked about Mommy?"

"Not exactly. But they did talk about remodeling the two rooms on the third floor of their brownstone for the kids, and also discussed enrolling them in a private school as soon as the trial is over."

Blair laughed shortly and Jan thought that he was probably embarrassed by his client's indiscretion.

"I realize you've instilled your client with a great deal of confidence in your abilities, Blair," she went on, "but I think he should be a little more careful about how he handles the children. After all, you and I agreed at the pretrial conference that John and Carole should discuss the case with the children as little as possible."

"Okay, you're right. I'll put a call in to John and get his side of the story. If Carole's version is right, I'll give him hell. Will that take care of it?"

"I'm sure it will," Jan answered agreeably.

"While we're on the subject of the Downing case, have you heard from Judge Miller?" Blair asked.

"I have a message that she called, but I haven't gotten back to her yet. Why?"

"You're going to love this one. She's requesting that we get the Downings together and see if we can accomplish anything, clarify any of the issues. Of course, she's hoping that we can get them to agree to something, so that she can lighten her calendar load, but there's not much chance of that."

"No, it's not very probable that either one of them will give in. What shall we do about the conference?"

"Hold it, I guess. Do we really have a choice? When Judge Miller makes a 'suggestion,' it always sounds like an order to me."

"Okay," Jan answered, "just tell me where and when, and I'll set it up with Carole."

"Let's try for your office, Monday at ten o'clock. I'll call John when I hang up here, and unless he can't make it, it's on."

"Of course," Jan answered, biting her lip to hold back the angry words that were on the tip of her tongue. Blair wasn't even asking her to check her calendar, or to check with Carole and see if she was free. If he and John could make it, the "girls" were expected to be there.

"Can we get together tonight?" Blair asked.

"Actually, I was calling to invite you to dinner."

"I'd love dinner. But don't bother to cook. I'll take you out to eat. I know a great little Italian place."

"No, I'd rather you came to my place tonight," Jan answered sweetly.

"I get the feeling you're insisting on feeding me tonight because I fed you last night. Because you don't like to be obligated to me."

"I'm sorry you have that feeling." The sound of his deep, sensuous voice was unnerving to her, making her less and less sure of her motives. But the damned Downing case was also bringing out her competitive spirit. It was juvenile of her to try and get the best of Blair in every situation, just to prove that she was his equal. She knew that, and Blair seemed to know what she was up to. But, just this one night, she wanted to outdo him, to have him at her mercy, to show him just what kind of competitor he was up against.

"Are you going to try and find a better Chinese restaurant, so you can show me up in my own court?" he asked, obviously enjoying himself.

"Blair, this is really ridiculous."

"You bet it is. But I have the feeling that soon

I'm going to run out of ways to keep a step ahead of you."

"That's absurd, Blair. Listen, I have to run. Let me know if you can make it tonight."

"I can make it," he answered quickly. "Around seven?"

"Fine, see you then."

Jan had started to replace the receiver when the sound of Blair's voice made her carry it back to her ear just in time to hear him say, "Hey, I love you." The gentle tone of his voice and the wonder of his simple declaration warmed Jan's heart.

"Me, too," she murmured. Then she hung up and, pulling a legal pad toward her, began to make her plans for the evening.

By working hard all afternoon and skipping a well-deserved coffee break, Jan managed to get out of the office a few minutes early. She stopped at the market for steaks, fresh broccoli, and salad vegetables. She bought a box of strawberries, out of season and exorbitantly priced, then hurried home to spread the dining-room table with her best lace tablecloth. She laid two place settings of delicate bone china, added gleaming silver and aromatic candles in silver holders. The final touch was the sparkling crystal goblets inherited from her grandmother.

She tossed the salad, made a delicate cheese sauce for the broccoli, and whipped cream for the strawberries. Then she heated the broiler for the steaks and took a tray of frozen dinner rolls from the freezer to pop in the oven at the last minute.

After a quick shower, she dressed in a shimmering lavender at-home outfit that clung seductively to her firm breasts and hugged her small waist. She brushed out her long gleaming hair and touched her cheeks with a hint of blush. She sprayed her pulse points liberally with her favorite expensive scent. She knew that Blair would find her desirable, and she trembled with anticipation.

When it was time for Blair to arrive, she dimmed the lights in the living room, lit the candles on the table, and put a stack of records on the stereo turntable. The gentle voice of her favorite male singer filled the room, and Jan, resplendent in her long lavender gown, floated through the apartment, putting the finishing touches to the perfect seductive setting.

When Blair walked into the apartment and took her into his arms, the look on his face told Jan that she had planned everything just right. He narrowed his green eyes to take in the dimly lit room, fragrant with the mixed odors of good food and burning candles. His glance lingered on the stereo turntable, spinning gently around and around as it emitted the strains of a popular love song.

"If I was a confirmed bachelor," he told Jan, "I'd run for my life."

"I don't know what you mean," she answered, looking up at him through lowered lashes.

"You know very well what I mean." Blair smiled. "I mean this room. And you. You're turning into quite a seductress."

"Don't tell me you don't like being seduced, Mr. Wynter," Jan purred.

"I haven't had too much experience along those lines, but I think I'm going to like it fine. Still, I can't help but wonder what you're up to."

"You have a very suspicious mind," Jan said as she took his jacket.

"Maybe I just like to be sure I'm being seduced for the right reasons."

"Meaning?"

"What I mean is, is it me you're wooing tonight, or the lawyer who represents John Downing?"

"Both," Jan answered unhesitatingly. "I'm trying to convince both of you of my qualifications."

"Then you're wasting your time. The personal part of me is already convinced, and the professional part of me isn't open to bribery."

She took his hand and led him toward the couch. "Relax and I'll bring you a glass of wine, then I'll put the steaks under the broiler."

"I don't believe this," Blair murmured as he followed her docilely to the couch. "All this, just because I ordered Chinese last night."

"Uh-huh," Jan answered, "you didn't know what you were letting yourself in for, did you?"

"That's all right. I love surprises."

When Blair was ensconced on one end of the long couch, Jan brought his chilled wine, then returned to the kitchen to finish preparing their dinner. When she came back, he was sitting with his eyes closed, a dreamy expression on his face.

"Why don't we get married right away, Jan?" he asked when he sensed her presence in the room.

"Is that your idea of a romantic proposal, 'Why don't we get married right away, Jan?'" She laughed to cover the thudding of her heart.

"We've talked about marriage," Blair said, opening his eyes and gazing at her speculatively. "Maybe I didn't make a romantic proposal, but we both know where we're heading, don't we?"

Jan felt the familiar warmth begin to spread through her chest, into her stomach, down her legs. She wanted nothing more than to sit beside Blair on the couch and fall into his strong arms. But she remained standing a couple of feet away from him, somehow afraid of this total commitment he was offering.

"It wouldn't be like this every night, you know," she said, playing the devil's advocate. "You'd probably be lucky if you got this kind of treatment once a month. Most nights you'd be foraging for yourself or stopping off for a pizza on your way home from the office."

"But I'd still have the nights like this to look forward to, wouldn't I?" Blair asked.

"Yes, I guess you would." Jan's attitude softened, as she watched his eyes hungrily devour her. "You have it now," she added, "you don't have to marry me."

"But I want it in writing," he teased. "On the back of a marriage certificate."

"You'll get it," Jan promised. "But we have a few things to work out first."

"Such as?" He lifted his sandy brows over his cool green eyes questioningly.

"Such as our priorities. And right now, my top priority is for the steak in the broiler."

She ran back to the kitchen and turned the steaks, then leaned on the counter and breathed deeply until her pounding heart began to beat normally again.

Blair wanted to marry her, and she wanted nothing in the world more than to belong to him. But she knew that it would be a mistake to let him rush her into it. She needed time to sort things out, to convince him of the importance of her career. She needed to finish up the Downing case and see what the future held for her. There was no way that she could just drop everything and abandon her dream to open her own office. As much as Blair meant to her, she couldn't do that. Yes, time was what she needed, and time was what Blair would just have to give her.

"Hey, are those steaks about done? I'm starving," Blair called from the living room. The sound of his voice brought a smile to Jan's lips and a new strength to her resolve. She loved Blair Wynter and she wasn't about to give him up again. As she transferred the sizzling steaks to a serving platter and carried them into the dining room, Jan had no doubt in her mind that she would manage to keep both her career and her love.

"Did you have a chance to talk to John today?" she asked later, as she measured coffee into the filter and added cold water from the tap.

Blair's look told her that there were other things he would rather talk about, but he answered her question. "Yes, I talked to him."

"Well?" Jan hated to have to force the issue, but Blair certainly wasn't giving out any free information.

"He says Carole's upset about nothing. He and Lisa merely tried to prepare the kids for the eventuality of their moving in with their father and stepmother. He says it was a very low-key conversation and the kids weren't the least bit upset by it. As a matter of fact, John intimated that they were kind of excited by the prospect of moving in with him."

"And you believed him?"

Blair didn't answer, just watched her, obviously trying to gauge her mood.

"Well, I don't," she went on. "Not for a minute. Those kids love their mother and it would be more than a little traumatic to take them away from her."

"They love their father, too," Blair answered. "And don't think that losing him hasn't been traumatic."

"Who do they have to blame for that? Carole didn't kick John out. He left of his own free will, remember?"

"Marriage is a contract, Jan. And when one party stops fulfilling his or her part of the contract, you can't always fault the other party for walking."

"I agree with you that marriage is a contract. But the old-fashioned idea that a wife has to obey her husband's every whim just doesn't work anymore. And that's what John Downing wanted from Carole, absolute obedience."

"As far as the marriage vows go, Jan, what would you suggest, to just cut the word 'obey' from the ceremony?"

"You've been living in the Dark Ages, Blair. Hardly anyone says that these days. A lot of people are even writing their own vows so that they can say what they want to say to each other, not what some outdated male-oriented society set down a hundred years ago."

Blair shook his head and regarded Jan with amusement. "You're just not the old-fashioned girl I'd hoped to take home to Mother, are you?"

"You bet I'm not!"

"You know what I think?" Blair asked. He took her slim hand and turned it over slowly, then leaned to kiss the smooth palm. The touch of his lips sent a thrill up Jan's arm and her breath caught in her throat. "I think there's some of that old-fashioned girl in Janelle Richmond, cleverly hiding beneath that smooth, city-girl facade."

"Oh? What makes you think that?"

"Several things. In a way, you're so much the Girl Scout. Naïve, trusting, always looking for the good in people."

"You said that before. You also said that I'm

competitive and you insinuated that I'm too ambitious for a woman. You're not very consistent, are you?"

"Whoever told you consistency was a virtue?" he asked. He reached behind her and switched off the coffeepot, then pulled her into his arms. Jan's back was pressed against the kitchen counter as Blair leaned against her, his maleness hard against her thighs.

"I want you," he whispered into the softness of her throat. He nuzzled her neck and caressed her shoulders through the silky fabric of her gown.

"This isn't fair," Jan murmured. "I was supposed to seduce you." She wound her arms around his neck and ran her fingers through the soft hair at the back of his neck. When her cool fingers grazed his neck, he shivered and raised his shoulders.

"Your hands are cold," he explained.

"But my heart is warm," Jan answered, as she, too, shivered with anticipation.

"I'll warm your hands," Blair said, his voice low and tender. "I'll make you think it's spring again."

Warmth surged through Jan's body in response to his promise until she was on fire with desire for him. Her feeling for him was overpowering her, but she made one last feeble attempt to resist his advances. After all, wasn't this supposed to be *her* night, wasn't *she* supposed to be seducing *him?*

"I'm trying to make coffee, Blair," she said, pushing at him and halfheartedly trying to wiggle out of his embrace.

"We don't need coffee," he grumbled. Then he leaned across her and hit the switch that controlled the lights, throwing the kitchen into near darkness. Quickly, roughly, his mouth covered hers before she had a chance to protest his actions. "Is that

enough to convince you that I need you?" he asked
minutes later when they were both breathing
heavily.

"Never enough," she murmured. "Never . . . never
enough."

They clung to each other as they made their way
down the hallway to Jan's bedroom. "I love you,"
Blair whispered as they undressed quickly in the
dim light of the bedside lamp, devouring each other's
bodies with their eyes.

"And I love you," Jan answered, absolutely sure.
Then Blair opened his arms and she stepped into
them.

Hours later, when she had seen a happy, sleepy
Blair to the door, Jan sat down in front of her
dressing table and brushed out her long brown hair.
Her mind went back to a conversation they had had
earlier in the evening, when they were discussing
John and Carole Downing.

"You really want to win this one, don't you?"
Blair had asked in an accusing tone.

"I want to win *all* of them," she had answered,
knowing that she was avoiding a direct answer. It
was true that she wanted to win the Downing case
more than any other case she had ever handled, but
her mind was no longer so clear on the issue of *why*
that particular case was so important to her. Her
attitude toward John and Carole Downing had gotten all mixed up with her feelings about Blair. The
Downings' situation was one that she and Blair
could easily fall into, and she sometimes felt that
resolving Carole's case would resolve a conflict in
her own life.

She didn't actually feel that she would be compelled to choose between Blair and her career as a
lawyer. It wasn't that simple. But either marriage

or her career would have to be put on HOLD for a while, and Blair wanted to get married right away. He was the kind of man who wanted a wife and children, who wanted dinner on the table every night at six. Jan wondered if he would ever be content with the kind of gypsy existence he would surely have living with her.

There would be nights when she got home late, nights when she didn't have the time or the energy to talk, entire weeks when they would rarely see each other if one of them was in trial. Of course, Blair's life would be just as hectic as hers. He had gladly chosen a lawyer's life for himself, but Jan couldn't help but wonder if he would be as objective about his wife's career and the demands it made on their marriage.

"But you especially want to win this one," Blair had said earlier in the evening. "And, if you win, that means I'll lose. One of us has to lose. And what's going to happen to our relationship then, when one of us has to accept defeat at the other's hands?"

Well, Jan thought as she continued to run the brush through her hair, leave it to Blair to come up with a new wrinkle. What would happen when the case was over and one of them was the loser? It was certainly something to consider.

Jan blushed, and she was glad she was in the privacy of her own bedroom as she realized the reason she had never taken the time to consider that particular aspect of the case as a problem. It was because she didn't intend to lose, so she had only thought about how she would react to winning. Well, it was a great attitude to have and one she intended to keep. She would worry about losing later. Now, Blair's participation in the Downing case only heightened her desire to win, and the desire to win the case only heightened her desire to best Blair at all the other games people in love play.

Chapter Nine

Saturday was a typical cold, windy day in mid-October. Jan had just jumped out of the shower when the phone rang. She ran into the bedroom with a lime-and-green-striped towel wrapped around her dripping body. Even before she lifted the receiver, she knew it was Blair, and her heartbeat accelerated in anticipation of the sound of his voice.

"Where are we going?" Jan asked a couple of minutes later, when he had told her to wear jeans and dress warmly.

"It's a surprise."

"I hate surprises."

"You'll love this one. I'll pick you up in half an hour. Be ready."

Before she could protest further, the line went dead and Jan rushed to follow Blair's orders, not for a minute admitting to herself that that was what she was doing. Forty minutes later, he was hustling her onto a dirty, nearly empty subway train. When they exited at Battery Park, she thought she knew what he had in mind and she had to laugh at his ingenuity.

"I told you you'd love it. How many New Yorkers take pleasure cruises on the Staten Island Ferry?" he asked, guiding her down the ramp to the waiting boat.

"I don't have the statistics handy, but I would imagine the answer is 'not many.'"

"Smart girl. Well, we're going to be tourists today and do everything New Yorkers miss out on."

"I suppose, if I survive this, the Statue of Liberty's next?" she asked.

"Actually, I had that planned for next weekend."

Jan returned his smile and the pressure of his hand on hers. Standing at the rail on the deserted, windswept deck would have been exhilarating even if Blair hadn't been standing so close to her, his warmth shielding her from the worst of the cold autumn wind.

"This is wonderful," she told him, loving the swaying motion of the old boat that rocked her back and forth in his arms.

"You bet it is. All those poor people sitting inside on those hard little benches don't know what they're missing."

Jan laughed and snuggled closer to his chest. His arms hugged her to him as the deck rose and fell beneath their feet.

"Are you cold?" Blair asked, tilting her head to kiss her chilled lips.

"No," she answered, thinking that there were all kinds of cold and warmth and that maybe she would never be cold again.

"I'm not either. As a matter of fact, if all those people weren't staring at us from their warm, little haven, I'd probably try to undress you and make love to you right here."

He unzipped her stadium jacket, slid his hand inside, and massaged her breasts. The shock of cold air that hit her chest was quickly replaced by a surge of heat that came from deep inside of her.

"Blair, stop that," she protested feebly. "They all think we're crazy now."

"I am crazy," he answered. "Have been since the first time I saw you. Why do you think I let you win that stupid race?"

"You *what?*" Jan jerked away from him and zipped her jacket against a sudden cold breeze.

"Come on, you don't think you could really beat me, do you?" His look of surprise was so genuine that it didn't take Jan more than a heartbeat to figure it out. It was a game, and Blair thought that she had been playing it with him. He had let her beat him running that first morning so that they could meet, and all this time he had just assumed that she knew it, that she had been playing the game, too.

"You really thought you beat me, didn't you?" he asked incredulously, the corners of his mouth turning up into a grin.

"You can just wipe that stupid grin off your face," Jan told him, halfway between anger and helpless laughter.

"You're not used to losing, I can see that. I should never have opened my big mouth."

"Oh, of course, that would have been ideal. God, you're an impossible male chauvinist. Just let the little woman think she won, if that will make her happy. That idea smacks of the same attitude that believes in keeping women pregnant in the summer and barefoot in the winter."

"Not a bad idea."

Jan was trying hard not to give in to her innate good sense of humor. After all, she had been awfully stupid not to see through his subterfuge. What was it she had thought when he first passed her? *A real runner.* Then why in the world had she ever thought that she could outrun him? Blair was laughing so hard at the spectacle of outraged womanhood Jan presented that there were tears running down his cheeks.

"Stop that." She threw a punch at him, but he took advantage of her nearness and pulled her into his arms again. Quickly, his laughter died down and his mood turned serious.

"I'd never lie to you, Jan, or do anything to hurt you. I thought you knew all along, honest to God, I did. Forgive me for underestimating you?"

"Actually, I think you were *over*estimating me. But you're forgiven." She snuggled into his arms and finally allowed herself to see the humor in the situation. "It is kind of funny," she admitted. "I guess I'm more naïve than I thought. I'll have to watch that."

"You don't have to watch anything. I love you just the way you are." Blair's lips silenced her mouth and stilled the conflicting thoughts and emotions that swirled through her mind as the dirty green waters of New York Harbor swirled beneath the ferry. She was mortified that she had fallen for such an old, chauvinist trick. No wonder he thought she was naïve!

Yet, no matter what the circumstances, she was glad she had met Blair. And she couldn't deny that the situation was an amusing one. Well, there was nothing to be done about it now. She would just have to be more careful in the future, and when she beat him at anything, she would have to be sure that her victory was not a pacifying gift from Blair.

When they got back to Manhattan, they shopped together for groceries, then holed up in Jan's apartment for the rest of the day. But when evening began to fall, Blair suggested that maybe they should get out of the apartment and go out for dinner.

Jan jumped up from the couch and headed for the telephone extension in the kitchen. "How about the Top of the Park?"

"Fine," Blair answered.

"I'll phone for reservations," Jan said, the phone already in her hand.

"You're a real take-charge lady, aren't you?" Blair asked from the doorway.

"Does that bother you?" When Blair hesitated before answering, Jan smiled her amusement. "It *could* bother you, couldn't it?"

"Yes, maybe it could. I don't like to be bossed around."

"Am I bossing you around?" she asked, not quite so amused.

"Not exactly. But I think you would be capable of it."

"And you wouldn't like that, because I'm a woman. If I was just one of the boys, though, it wouldn't make any difference if I was the take-charge type, if I just went ahead and called in reservations without consulting you first."

"I'm not planning on spending the rest of my life with one of the boys, Jan."

"Well, if you're planning on spending it with a woman, you'd better learn how to be a little more tactful."

"And who's going to teach me tact, you?"

Jan's eyes flashed blue fire, but the dangerous moment passed quickly and soon her expression softened. Her eyes sparkled with mirth as she considered Blair's question.

"That would be like the blind leading the blind, wouldn't it?" she asked.

"You can say that again." Blair smiled easily, but his relief was evident. If he had been expecting Jan to continue the argument, he didn't know how close he had come to a sampling of her temper.

The rest of the evening went smoothly, with neither of them courageous enough to bring up the Downing case again. Blair had made plans to drive down to the Jersey shore and watch a marathon on Sunday, so when he left her at the door after dinner, they agreed that they would not see each other again until Monday at the conference with the Downings.

On Sunday morning, Jan finished up the work she had brought home from the office and straightened her apartment. By noon, she wished she had accompanied Blair to the marathon. He had invited her, but she had turned down the invitation. At the time, she thought it might do them good to spend the day apart. In the afternoon, she cleaned out the huge walk-in closet in her bedroom and rearranged her dresser drawers, passing time until Monday, when she would see Blair again.

She turned on the stereo, and every love song seemed to have been written for them. She picked up a novel, and the hero reminded her of Blair. Everything she did brought him closer to her and she pictured him driving to the shore, standing in the crowd watching the runners.

By nine o'clock in the evening, she had showered and wrapped herself in her cranberry velour robe. She hadn't bothered to dry her hair with the blow dryer and it hung damply to her shoulders. She shivered and turned up the heat in the living room before she settled on the white leather couch with a volume of constitutional law. But it held no interest for her, and she soon laid it aside and picked up a new historical novel. Strains of Vivaldi wafted from the stereo in the background. She promised herself a cup of mocha tea and bed by eleven, no matter how interesting the novel proved to be. She was determined to get a good night's sleep, so that she would be in good shape to start the week the following morning.

When the bell rang to announce that she had a caller waiting downstairs, Jan felt a quick stab of fear. No one just dropped by to see her at nine o'clock in the evening without telephoning first.

The bell rang again, a long, insistent keening that propelled Jan off the couch and across the room. She pushed the door release to let her caller into the lobby, then waited until she heard the elevator doors hiss open. She stared into the tiny peephole in the door and saw Blair's distorted face, his green eyes staring straight at her. She cracked the door to make sure that it was really him before opening it wide to admit him. But he didn't come in. He just stood there in the hallway looking at Jan with a strange smile on his handsome face. His eyes took in her slippered feet, the fluffy velour robe, the soft dark hair that hung in wet tendrils across her slim shoulders, the lovely face completely free of makeup.

"I'm sorry, I didn't know you were coming by," she apologized. "I just took a shower and I—" Her hand moved to the front of the robe and held it together. She was beginning to feel uncomfortable, the way he was just standing there, staring at her, not making any move to enter the apartment.

"Don't apologize," he said finally. "You look beautiful."

Their eyes locked and held and a current of electricity shot through Jan's blood. Touch me, her eyes said, and Blair reached out with his right hand. In it, he held a single long-stemmed red rose.

"I know I told you I wouldn't come by tonight," he said, "but when I saw this rose, it reminded me of you. Once I was reminded of you, I couldn't stop thinking about you. So here I am, with my humble offering." He handed her the rose and watched while she brought it close to her face and inhaled its subtle fragrance, then twirled it slowly in her slender fingers, admiring its perfect beauty.

"Thank you. It's beautiful."

"There were a lot of them on the cart but this one stood out in the crowd. I knew that it had to be yours." His voice was husky with emotion and Jan knew that, although he was talking about the lovely, delicate rose, he was thinking about her standing so close to him, fresh from the shower, naked beneath the robe that she held together with trembling hands.

"Come in," she said, stepping back to give him space to squeeze around her. They were barely inside when he reached for her, drawing her into his arms. His long, sensitive fingers gently kneaded her back as he pressed her body to his. His lips lingered on her forehead, her cheek, and finally, her waiting lips. His lips warmed hers and the gentle heat spread slowly through her body. He shifted his weight and moved his body against hers, sending small shivers of pleasure through every part of her body as it made contact with his. She was aware of the hard strength of him, the arms that held her, the legs that rubbed against her bare ones beneath the cranberry robe.

Blair slipped his jacket from his shoulders and dropped it on the floor behind him, and Jan smiled, thinking again how good he was at doing things without taking his hands off her for a minute. She slid her hands up beneath his brown polo shirt and he immediately moved his hands from her back and slipped them beneath her robe, to touch her breasts. She sighed deeply and pushed herself into his hands as he freed her breasts from the confines of the robe. She moaned aloud as he lowered his head and sucked her already erect nipples. Her body was ready for him and she felt that she would soon burst from the pressure building inside of her. Her breasts were swollen, her nipples extended, and when he finally removed his lips, she almost cried out at the loss.

"I want you, Jan."

"I know you do. I want you, too."

He laughed and nuzzled her neck. "I guess the feeling is completely mutual tonight."

"It always has been, ever since the first time."

He lifted her as easily as if she were a child and carried her down the hall to her bedroom, where she had already turned down the bed for her solitary night's sleep. He raised his eyebrows and smiled when he saw that the bed was ready. He laid her in the middle of the cool blue sheets and quickly removed his own clothing before he knelt on the bed beside her. She reached out for the switch to turn off the small light she had left burning beside her bed, but he stopped her. "No, I want to see you. I want to watch you."

In the dim light from the single lamp he traced the lines of her face, then the contours of her body. His eyes studied her and consumed her as his fingers teased and explored. He moved from her rounded breasts to her slim waist, from her flat stomach to her long legs and shapely thighs. Finally, he dared to touch the center of her sexuality, to twist his fingers in her dark, curly hair.

Jan shuddered and reached out for him, urging him to take her quickly. Still, he lingered over her, moving slowly to kneel between her parted thighs, bending to touch with his lips the places his fingers had touched. Jan was on fire with longing, bursting with desire for him. When she thought she couldn't stand it another minute, he finally entered her. He moved slowly up and down, in and out, setting a perfect, easy rhythm that she followed with the movement of her body beneath his.

She strained upward in an effort to touch every part of him with a part of herself, to cling to him every moment until he released her. Her breasts pressed flat against his solid chest, her stomach adhered to his, her long legs wound around him to hold him captive. She buried her face in his neck and moved her lips along the contours of his jaw. His arms were around her, beneath her, pulling her closer and closer as they moved together in an accelerating rhythm as old as mankind.

"I love you, Jan." The words were whispered softly into her hair. So softly that, a moment after they were spoken, she wondered if she had dreamed them. She longed to tell Blair that she loved him, too, as she had told him many times before. But she was afraid. The moment was too rawly physical and too magically unreal. "Love me, Blair," she murmured instead, and he answered her, "Yes. Oh, yes."

He quickened the rhythm of his thrusts and drove deeper and deeper inside her. Her back ached from the pressure of his arms that bound her to him, but the pain was nothing compared to the pleasure that was fast overtaking her.

They reached the moment of fulfillment together,

in a great, tender, fiery explosion. Lights exploded in her head as she felt tremor after ecstatic tremor course through her body. Her heart beat frighteningly fast, her chest heaved, her legs and arms trembled uncontrollably. It was the most beautiful moment that she had ever experienced. Blair rolled over and they lay side by side, spent and drained. Still, when his arms reached for her again, Jan rolled eagerly into them, wanting him still.

Chapter Ten

On Monday morning, Jan tried to put Blair out of her mind and concentrate all of her energies on her work. But she couldn't easily forget about him for more than a few minutes at a time. Memories of the night before kept flooding into her mind, bringing a smile to her lips and a blush to her cheeks, even though she was alone in her apartment.

By nine o'clock, whe was sitting behind the modern L-shaped desk in her office, thinking about the Downing case. Something had been nagging at the back of her mind all weekend. She knew that something wasn't right with the case, but she couldn't put her finger on the problem. Then, all at once, she knew what it was. It was Carole's attitude. Carole was an intelligent woman, a sharp businesswoman. She was making her own way in the competitive business world against staggering odds. If there was one thing Carole had, it was guts. It seemed to Jan that it was out of character for Carole to be so frightened of losing her children to her exhusband. Unless she had a good reason for her fear, a reason that she had not yet confided to her attorney.

Suddenly sure that there was something important Carole hadn't told her, Jan paced the floor of her office until Carole arrived at nine-thirty.

"Come in and sit down, Carole. I'll ask Barbra to bring us some coffee."

Carole nodded gratefully and Jan buzzed Barbra to request coffee and danish, then settled herself behind her desk. Carole smiled warmly and relaxed in the chair she had taken across the desk from Jan.

"Oh, Jan, you don't know how nervous I am. It's been so long since I've talked to John face to face. I don't know exactly how I'm going to react to him. I'm so damned afraid he's going to get custody of the kids."

"That's what I want to talk to you about," Jan replied. "Oh, here's our coffee. Thanks, Barbra."

Usually Barbra's attitude showed signs of resentment when Jan asked her to bring coffee to clients. Barbra was a top-notch legal secretary and she felt that her duties did not include providing coffee and snacks for clients. Jan agreed with her and only very rarely requested this service. And Barbra always knew that, a day or so after performing such a "degrading" service, she would be sent home early in the afternoon or granted a double lunch hour to go shopping with a friend or just about anything else that she requested, within reason.

Today, however, Barbra showed no sign of resentment when she was requested to bring coffee. She smiled as she brought the two mugs of coffee to Jan's desk and even commented that she had brewed a fresh pot and that the cheese danish were delicious. Jan knew what was going on. Barbra felt sorry for Carole Downing and sympathized with her situation.

When Barbra had left the office, Jan delved right in.

"Carole," Jan said, "I have a terrible feeling that we're going to lose our case." Jan realized that she was exaggerating, but she knew she had to impress Carole with the seriousness of their situation. "I've gone over the file a dozen times, and for the life of me, I can't figure out what's wrong. But something *is* wrong. So there must be something that I don't know, because my instincts are usually on target and right now they tell me that we're in trouble. Do you have any idea what that something might be?"

"I don't know," Carole answered vaguely, avoiding eye contact with Jan.

"Well, try to think what John could have to use against you. Are you dating someone he would seriously disapprove of, someone of questionable character who might be a threat to the children's well-being?"

"No, of course not," Carole mumbled, staring down at her lap.

"Then how about drugs? Do you ever smoke pot? Believe me, I hate to have to ask you these questions, but we have a lot at stake here. All right, then, how about alcohol?" Jan could see from the shocked look on Carole's face that she had hit a nerve. And her own reaction was one of shock, too. She would never have suspected Carole of being a drinker.

"Oh, Jan, I'm so ashamed," Carole cried, tears filling her blue eyes and overflowing down her cheeks. "You trusted me, and I didn't want to betray your trust. I wanted to tell you everything, but I was so ashamed. I wasn't sure that John knew and I thought maybe it wouldn't even come up at the trial. Does he know, is that what you're trying to tell me?"

"Carole, I'm not sure how much John knows, but why don't you start at the beginning and tell me exactly what's been going on." One thing Jan knew for sure was that her philosophy was working again.

If you trusted your clients, they would come through with the truth, sooner or later.

"I've got a drinking problem, Jan. Not a serious one," Carole added hastily. "When John walked out, I started having a couple of glasses of wine after dinner, just to help me through the lonely nights. Then, as the pressure of my business built up, the after-dinner drinks turned into something stronger."

"Just how serious is your problem now Carole?" Jan asked sympathetically.

"I'm not an alcoholic or anything like that. But I guess the kids must have mentioned it to John. Knowing John, he probably built it up all out of proportion."

"Are you getting any professional help?" Jan asked, her mind racing with ideas.

"No. I told you, it's not that serious."

"Believe me, Carole, if it's serious enough to make you think John could use it to take your children away from you, it's serious enough to require professional help."

"I just don't know if I can face that, Jan. It would be so humiliating. And what would the children think?"

"John and Missy love you, Carole. I think they'd be happy to see you trying to cure your problem."

"You're right, of course." Carole sat very still, staring down at her hands, which were clenched in her lap. "You know, Jan, I hate to admit it, but sometimes I wonder if it was worth it."

Jan didn't answer, but she hoped that Carole would go on. Jan was the woman's lawyer, but they were also becoming friends and she wanted to encourage Carole's confidence. Carole was not basically a strong woman, and Jan knew that it had taken a lot of nerve for her to face up to her domineering husband and demand her rights. Jan admired Carole's courage and her quick intelligence and hoped that their friendship would continue after the lawsuit was a thing of the past.

"I've gained a lot since the morning I woke up with the realization that my life was empty and that I'd have to make some changes if I wanted to retain my sanity," Carole went on. "But I've had some heavy losses, too."

"You mean John?" Jan asked, trying to draw Carole out.

"Yes, John, for one. I loved him so much, Jan. I still miss him sometimes. I probably always will. You don't know how it hurt when he married Lisa. But there's more to it than just the loss of John himself. In gaining my independence, I've sometimes felt as though I've lost another part of myself. I guess I'm trying to say that sometimes I don't feel very feminine anymore. Maybe that's why the drinks after dinner help. It isn't easy to lie in bed alone night after night, after being married for twelve years."

"Carole, you're a very attractive woman." Jan wondered how Carole could not be more confident of that herself; she was tall and stately, with a good figure, had natural ash-blonde hair, wide blue eyes, and an engaging personality. "I can't imagine that you'd have any trouble finding a man."

"Oh, there's no problem there." Carole laughed. "But just any man isn't the answer, and you know it. I wish I could meet someone I could love who would accept me the way I am, both parts of me, the woman and the *person*. Oh, I'm probably not making any sense at all!"

"You're making a lot of sense," Jan assured her.

"And you will find someone, Carole, I'm sure of it. Just try to be patient. Love is one thing you can't hurry," Jan spoke from her own experience.

Carole laughed and raised her eyes to meet Jan's. "You know me pretty well, don't you, Jan? Once I decide I want something, I want it right away. Patience isn't one of my strong points."

"Well, I think being impatient is an integral ingredient of the ambitious man or woman. At least, that's what I keep telling myself."

"Are you trying to tell me that *you're* impatient, Jan? I can't believe that. You have such an easygoing disposition."

"That's the mask I wear for my clients, Carole," Jan joked. "Wait till you get to know me better. Now, I think we'd better get back to your problem. Do you have any ideas about counseling? Anyone you could call on for help?"

"I'm at a complete loss, Jan," Carole admitted.

"Okay, I can give you the name of a man I've used before. He specializes in alcohol and drug-related problems and he's experienced at testifying, if we feel that's necessary. I'll give him a call and ask him to slip you in for an initial consultation this week. Then he'll probably be able to see you several more times before the trial."

"I don't know how to thank you, Jan."

Jan waved her hand to dismiss the idea of thanks, even though her client's heartfelt gratitude meant more to her than the fee she would receive.

"Make sure you call him right away," she instructed Carole, "and be sure to keep the appointment. I can't impress upon you how important this is to your case. If we can show the judge that you're receiving voluntary help, nothing John says about your drinking will have as much impact. And one more thing: don't tell anyone that you're going for counseling, not even John and Missy. We'll tell them after the trial. Right now, let it be our secret."

Having settled the matter of the counselor, Jan waited in her office talking with Carole about nothing in particular until Barbra stuck her head in the door. "Mr. Wynter is here with Mr. Downing. Shall I show them in?"

"Give us two or three minutes first, Barbra, then bring them in," Jan answered.

When Barbra had closed the door again, Jan turned to Carole. "Now don't be nervous. As I already explained to you, we're having this conference because the judge recommended it. I don't really expect to settle anything today. Both of you want custody of the children and it's not very likely that either of you will change your mind within the next hour."

"Then why put us through this, Jan?" Carole asked. "I'm a nervous wreck."

"Just try to relax and don't get angry, no matter what they say. I don't think they'll bring up your drinking problem. They'll probably save that to spring on us at the trial. This can't hurt us and it just might give us a better indication of what we're up against."

"Okay." Carole sighed and settled into her chair as the door opened and Barbra admitted Blair and John Downing.

"Hello, Blair. Mr. Downing." Jan stood and indicated two chairs directly in front of her desk. She had moved Carole off to the right, where she would be separated from the two men by the space of a few feet. Although Jan intended to try and keep the conference peaceable, she had once been witness to a meeting of this type that had suddenly erupted into physical violence. So, just in case, she was taking the precaution of keeping Carole safely out of her ex-husband's reach.

As she once again explained the reason for the conference and what they hoped to accomplish, Jan let her eyes travel back and forth between the three people seated across from her. Carole and John were studiously ignoring each other, both watching Jan carefully, as though they felt they could get some extra meaning from her words by studying her facial expressions. Blair, too, was staring at her, the hint of a smile playing on his lips and in his eyes.

Jan wished that she had planned to see him alone for a minute before their clients were admitted to the room. She could have sent Carole down to the conference room for a few minutes, so that she and Blair could have been alone together. It was hard to see him this way and not be able to touch him. A quick hug and a kiss or two would certainly have made it easier to face the next hour. She smiled at the thought, but quickly wiped the smile from her face when she became aware of the Downings' puzzled expressions.

Blair cleared his throat and took over where Jan left off. "You've read our petition and I don't think there's anything in it that requires an explanation. John wants custody of the children and he feels that this would be in the children's best interests. He would be perfectly willing to work out a viable arrangement with Carole to give her generous visitation rights. Maybe we should start by discussing Carole's feelings about this."

"Obviously," Jan said, "Carole has no intention of giving up her custodial rights. If she did, we wouldn't be planning to go to trial on this."

"Well," Blair broke in, "the judge wants us to at least discuss it, Jan."

"We'll be only too glad to discuss. If John wants to drop his petition and allow Carole to retain custody, I'm sure we can work out suitable visitation rights for *him*."

John Downing leaned forward in his chair and spoke for the first time since entering the room. "This isn't getting us anywhere, Blair. I told you this would be a complete waste of time. I'm a busy man—"

"We all realize what a busy man you are, Mr. Downing," Jan broke in. "As a matter of fact, I imagine all of us could have found something else to occupy ourselves with this morning."

"Just a minute," Blair stood and began to pace back and forth across the room. He unbuttoned his jacket and loosened his tie, and Jan's breath caught in her throat as she suddenly remembered undoing buttons and helping him out of his clothes. His long, sensitive fingers played with the buttons of his jacket and Jan was mesmerized, remembering how his hands had felt on her body. She had a hard time pulling her eyes away from his hands and returning them to his face.

"I think we should go into what both John and Carole have to offer the children," Blair said, oblivious of Jan's feelings. "Obviously, they both love John, Jr. and Missy very much and both are able to give them a place to live. Is that much agreed?" Blair looked to both John and Carole for affirmation, before turning to face Jan.

"Of course, that's agreed," she answered.

"Then what we need to establish and discuss now is the quality of care the children are receiving now, and the quality of care they would receive if they lived with their father."

"Excuse me, but I don't understand this at all," Carole interrupted. "I mean, I think I understand what you're saying, but I can't believe it. I don't know what 'quality' has to do with custody of children. John has always felt that I, as their mother, should gladly bear the responsibility of taking care of them. He always told me that their care was my 'job.' So, I can't understand why he wants to take them away from me when he has always been very vocal about the fact that women were made to bear and raise children, while men were made to go out into the marketplace and earn their support. It seems to me that he's starting to contradict himself."

John Downing started to speak, but Blair shushed him with a wave of his hand and replied to Carole's statement himself.

"For the purpose of this conference, Mrs. Downing, I think it would be better to avoid making accusations. If we could reach some sort of a tentative agreement here, the petition would not have to be heard, and this could save all of us a lot of time and, possibly, a great deal of embarrassment. Also, the children would be spared—"

"Just a minute," Jan said. "I think it's unfair to talk to Carole about sparing the children's feelings. Your client should have thought of that before he filed the petition. Further, I think Carole has made a valid point that warrants discussion. For years, your client turned the care of the children over to his wife. John and Missy are great kids. They're well-mannered, polite, intelligent. I think we can safely assume that they have turned out this way due to Carole's influence. Now, all at once, Carole is being accused of being an unfit mother. That just isn't logical."

"If you read our petition, you must know that we aren't saying that Carole is incapable of raising children. But at this particular time, under these particular circumstances, we feel that John would be able to offer them a better quality of care. For one thing, Lisa would be able to give them constant supervision, which at their age is very important."

"Where does Lisa enter into this?" Jan asked, interrupting Blair's dialogue. "This is a custody suit between John and Carole. Lisa is not the natural mother of the children. I can't see how she could be expected to offer them the same degree of loving care that their natural mother could provide for them."

"We don't argue that, all other things being equal. But everything is not equal. Carole works long hours, she dates, she—"

"Are you saying that she shouldn't date? That she shouldn't be allowed to plan a future for herself? Have you ever heard the expression 'What's good for the goose is good for the gander'?"

"I've heard that," Blair answered with a grin, "but I don't think you'll find a New York statute to back it up."

"Seriously," Jan said, "it's bad enough that women have to put up with a double standard in their personal lives. But to find it in the law, too—or at least in your interpretation of the law—is completely unacceptable."

"I think you're purposely misinterpreting. I'm not trying to impose a double standard of morality on Carole. I'm saying, in the most simple language, that Carole does not have *time* to be a really good parent, considering the time she devotes to everything else."

"And I suppose 'everything else' includes her social life?" Jan asked.

"Nobody is implying that Carole should spend every minute of her time with her children. We're just saying that there are only so many hours in the day, and right at this particular point in time, Carole is spreading herself pretty thin. And it's the children who are suffering."

"I think we should let Johnny and Missy tell us how they feel about this," Carole put in before Jan had a chance to reply to Blair's accusations. John looked as if he wanted to agree with Carole's suggestion. But he probably wasn't sure if it would be wise to agree with his ex-wife on anything.

"Johnny and Missy have both indicated to their father that they'd like to see a little more of their mother than they do," Blair said.

"Is that true, John?" Carole asked, turning toward her ex-husband, her pretty face beginning to show the strain of the past half-hour.

John refused to meet her eyes, but he did give Carole the courtesy of an answer. "They've always felt that way, ever since you decided to go back to school. You, of all people, should know that."

"All right, let me get this straight," Jan said, wisely taking the ball from the Downings before they started throwing accusations back and forth. "Your main complaint is that Carole doesn't spend enough time with the children. If she agreed to sell her business and stay home playing mommy all day, you would withdraw your petition and let her retain custody, is that right?"

John let out an exasperated sigh, but Blair was quick to answer. "The time element isn't our *only* concern, and we aren't asking that Carole sell her business. I think you're trying to paint this thing too black and white." He was glaring at Jan, his green eyes icily opaque.

"Yes, of course, I am," Jan answered. "Because cutting down her hours and working part-time would be disastrous to Carole, as would completely curtailing her social life. Of course, if she sold the business and stayed home at John's request, Judge Miller just might sign an order requiring him to pay alimony on top of the child support he's currently paying. Would your client be willing to support Carole in the manner to which she's become accustomed?"

"You're being ridiculous." From the incredulous look on John's face, he obviously agreed with his attorney. "We have never even suggested that Carole sell her business," Blair said.

"No," Jan answered, "but you have suggested that she give up her children. It sounds to me as if you're giving her a choice: her business or her children. And I'd simply like to know what your position will be if she chooses her children."

"We're obviously not getting any place here." Blair picked up his briefcase from the corner of the desk and motioned to John Downing that they were going to leave.

"No, we're not," Jan hurried to answer, "because your client doesn't want to compromise; he wants Carole's children."

"They're his children, too," Blair said, already moving toward the door with John Downing at his heels. With his hand on the doorknob, he turned and faced Jan and her client. "I think we can inform Judge Miller that a conference was held with a completely unsatisfactory outcome."

"That's the one thing we can agree on," Jan answered coldly.

A tearful Carole Downing left the office shortly after Blair and John. She was hardly out the door when Jan's phone rang.

"Jan Richmond," she answered wearily, drained by the emotional turn the conference had taken.

"Hi, it's me, your friendly adversary."

"Oh, Blair." She couldn't help but wish that he had waited to call until after she'd had a chance to separate what she felt about the Downing case from her own private emotions. Although Carole and John were unaware of it, there had been a lot more at stake in the conference than the resolution of their problems. She and Blair had actually been arguing out their own feelings, using the Downing case for a sounding board. Not very professional conduct for two attorneys.

"I love your enthusiasm," Blair said when it became evident that Jan was waiting for him to say something.

"Sorry," she answered, her weariness showing in her voice.

"Talkative, aren't you? You sound as if you're angry again."

"Not angry, just confused."

"Then what was that all about. I felt as if you were attacking me personally."

"You got the wrong impression. Actually, I was arguing for my client's rights," Jan hedged.

"Look, I'm just down in the lobby of your building. Let's have lunch and talk this thing out."

"I'm sorry, Blair, but I was planning on skipping lunch today. As a matter of fact, I think Mark is waiting to fill me in on another case I'll be handling."

"Okay, how about dinner, then?"

"I don't know for sure if I can make it. Can I call you later?"

"Sure, call me later," Blair answered dejectedly.

It wasn't that she didn't want to see Blair, because she did. She spent every moment away from him just waiting to be with him again, and the hour she had just spent, so close to him and yet so far away, had made her want him even more. It was just that she didn't want to argue with him, especially not when she was emotionally exhausted and she knew that they would have words about how the two of them had behaved at the conference. It was inevitable. She wanted to hold Blair, to kiss him, to laugh with him at their own private jokes. She wanted to forget the Downing case and the practice of law and everything else that might come between them. But it was foolish to think that their problems could be ignored. Blair was right—they had to talk, not about the Downings, but about themselves and their future.

She gave Blair time to get back to his office, then called him to accept his dinner invitation.

Chapter Eleven

They met at six at the Red Lion, a popular restaurant in the heart of the financial district. The large red-leather booths that lined one wall offered a sense of privacy to the diners that one couldn't find in some of the fancier restaurants.

Seated across from each other, their hands joined on the wooden tabletop, Jan again felt the magic that had touched her life since meeting Blair. She felt as if she were a special person, the way his eyes were drinking her in, the way his hand kept squeezing hers with a subtle pressure. Even without the use of words, Blair was able to let her know that he needed her and wanted her.

At moments like this, Jan realized what a depth of warmth and meaning Blair had brought into her life, and she silently resolved that she would do nothing that could result in losing him.

He waited until they had eaten before he turned the conversation to that morning's conference. "I guess we didn't accomplish much this morning, did we?" he asked, giving her an opening.

"I'm not even sure we were talking about John and Carole's problems half the time," Jan admitted.

"Let's be completely honest with each other, Jan. It wasn't a very professional way to treat our clients. I think we just about forgot they were in the room."

Jan laughed and reached for Blair's hand across the table. "I don't think it was so obvious to them. At least, I hope it wasn't."

"There are things we need to discuss, Jan. We've talked about marriage and we can't jump into something like that without knowing where we both stand."

"Suppose you tell me where you stand, Blair," Jan said, silently begging him to be reasonable.

"Well, since we keep using the Downing case as a parallel for our own feelings, I have to admit that I have a lot of sympathy for John. And I think Carole acted rather selfishly when she suddenly decided to go for a career. I also think that Johnny and Missy needed a mother more than New York City needed another interior decorator."

"Blair," Jan reasoned, "this afternoon you accused me of painting the picture too black and white. That's what you're doing now. Carole desperately needed an outlet for her individuality and her creativity. She needed that every bit as much as Johnny and Missy needed a mother. Anyway, she had no intention of depriving them of a mother. If John had just cooperated with her, there wasn't any reason why they couldn't have all been happy."

"I don't think Carole ever gave too much thought to John's happiness," Blair answered matter-of-factly.

"You're not being fair. You don't know what went on between them any better than I do. All we can do is take their word for it. From what Carole tells me, she loved John very much and was completely devastated by the divorce."

"She pushed him into it, Jan. She could have

backed down at any time and John would have gladly taken her back."

"Why did *she* have to be the one to back down? It seems to me he left no room for compromise then, just as he isn't now."

"Jan, what John was asking wasn't completely unreasonable. When he married Carole, she wanted to be a wife and a mother. She didn't have any big-deal plans, any world-shaking goals in life. If she had, they probably would never have married. Then, when the kids were still literally babies, she pops it on John that she's 'unfulfilled,' that she wants a career. Everything he had taken years to build started to fall down around John's head. His wife traipsed off to college with a bunch of kids almost half her age. His kids started coming down with mysterious illnesses, their grades started to fall. His own business started to suffer from his neglect. The poor guy thought he was going to lose it all."

"So the 'poor guy' solved all his problems by divorcing his wife and finding a woman who would star in his domestic fantasies," Jan finished for him.

Blair sighed and leaned back in the booth, releasing Jan's hand.

"Blair, they had been married twelve years and parented two children together. Don't you think he owed her something?" She leaned toward Blair, hoping to draw him back to her.

"You can't stay married to someone because you owe them, Jan. If it comes down to that . . ."

"Oh, I don't mean that he literally *owed* her, but if he had just given her a little consideration, they might have been able to work things out."

"Well, it's too late to worry about that now," Blair answered.

"Yes, I guess it is. But if we're talking about *us* and not the Downings, it's *not* too late."

"You know I'd never ask you to give up your career, Jan. I admire you and respect you too much for that." He leaned forward across the table, so close that she could feel his warm breath on her cheek.

"No, you might never ask me to do that in so many words."

"Meaning?"

"Meaning that you just might try to convince me without words."

"I won't pull a John Downing on you, Jan. If we *get* married, we'll *stay* married. I promise you that."

Jan decided not to carry the discussion any further, although she heartily disagreed with Blair that you could stay married by force of will. They were both tired tonight and she knew nothing would be gained by putting pressure on Blair to settle all of their problems in one night. But she wondered how he would react if she told him point-blank that her career was just as important to her as his career was to him. Well, she would find out soon enough, because she would definitely have to tell him before their relationship could progress much further.

When they left the restaurant, Blair hailed a cab and gave the address of his apartment.

"Wait a minute," Jan started to protest.

"Come home with me tonight," Blair whispered as he pulled her into his arms in the dark recesses of the cab. "I couldn't stand to be turned away at the door tonight."

"How do you know I was planning to turn you

away?" Jan asked as she sank into his arms and lifted her face to his.

"Because that's what you've been doing lately," Blair answered.

"I've never spent the night in a man's apartment. Anyway, I have to be in the office early in the morning."

But none of her excuses worked on Blair. "I didn't say you have to stay all night. I'll get you to work on time, don't worry about it."

When the cab pulled up in front of Blair's apartment building, Jan found that she was trembling uncontrollably. Going up in the antiquated elevator, she wished that she had insisted on going to her place. She didn't know why, but it seemed that she was making a commitment of some sort by going home with him. In her own apartment, on her own ground, she always had the upper hand. Now, she would be on his territory.

Blair let them into the apartment and locked the door firmly behind them.

"Coffee?" he asked. "Or a drink?"

"No," Jan answered, "nothing."

He took her coat and hung it in his hall closet, then sat down on the couch and waited for her to join him. When she did, he wrapped her in his arms and kissed her gently.

"Don't be so uptight," he said as his lips traced the soft curve of her ear. "Relax and let me love you. That's what you want to do, and you know it."

He unbuttoned her blouse and slipped his hands inside to caress her neck and her shoulders. The tension that had gripped Jan's insides started to melt away slowly as Blair's hands continued their gentle massage.

"Come on," Blair said finally, pulling her to her

feet. They crossed the hall to the bedroom and Blair opened a drawer and pulled out a pair of blue-striped pajamas. "The top is for you," he said, tossing it in her direction.

He went into the bathroom, carrying the pajama pants with him, and Jan shed her clothes and thrust her arms into the top. She was just buttoning it when Blair reentered the bedroom.

"Very sexy," he said, coming toward her. He reached her, but she pushed him away.

"Where do you keep your towels?" she asked. "I'd like to take a shower first, if you don't mind."

"There's a closet in the bathroom, well stocked by my weekly cleaning woman. Shampoo, toothpaste, washcloths—help yourself to anything you need."

"Your generosity is surpassed only by your sex appeal," she told him. He had sat down on the edge of the bed and she leaned over to plant a chaste kiss on the top of his head. She let her lips linger there as she pulled his head to her chest and slowly caressed his face with her hands.

"Hurry back," he urged, running a hand up her leg under the baggy pajama top and sending shivers of delight up and down her spine.

"Miss me," she answered, going into the bathroom and closing the door firmly behind her.

She heard music fill the bedroom as Blair turned on his stereo system, but it was quickly drowned out by the noise of the shower. She shampooed her long brown hair, then soaped her body luxuriously. As her hands followed the curves of her breasts and buttocks, she almost called out to Blair to join her. She imagined the sensation of his hands moving up and down her slick body and of how it would feel to run her soapy hands across his wide chest and his flat stomach. But she decided that it would be more fun to join him in the bed. She stepped out of the shower and, still dripping, wrapped herself in the huge brown bathsheet she had found in the linen closet.

Blair looked up as soon as the bathroom door opened and he watched, mesmerized, as Jan unwrapped the towel and let it slide to the floor. "Come here," he ordered.

"Say please," Jan countered, and he did. He said it with his lips and his eyes and his outstretched arms. Dripping water onto the deep beige shag carpet, she walked slowly toward the bed until she was standing above him.

"You look like a goddess risen from the sea." His words were a gentle caress that sent shivers of anticipation down her spine.

"I'm not a goddess," she whispered, "just a woman who needs you."

He lifted the blanket that now covered him and slid over to make room for her. But she refused the place at his side and sank down on top of him, spreading the length of her damp body on his. She pressed her cool breasts flat against his chest, coiled her long legs around his, then pressed her mouth against his and moved her body subtly, insinuatingly. She welcomed, as much as her own pleasure, the tremors that ran through Blair's body beneath hers.

"Let me—" Blair started to say, but Jan bit his lip and cut off his words.

"No way, it's my turn now. Just try to relax and enjoy it."

A sound escaped his lips that could have been either a protest or a moan of pleasure, and Jan was obsessed with a new kind of power that intoxicated her and drove her on. She moved her mouth to Blair's throat, then to his chest. She sucked at his nipples until they were as rigid as her own, then laid light, butterfly kisses down the length of his hard stomach. Her hands roamed his body, exploring it, glorying in the taut, firm skin over strong bone and muscle. She made love to him, returning the intensity he had shown when he was in command.

"Oh, Jan," Blair murmured, his eyes upon her lovely face, his hands running up and down her smooth back, then to her chest to cup and hold the fullness of her perfect breasts.

When she was ready, she reached down to guide him into her warm, sweet center. She moved rhythmically back and forth to her own inner drumbeat. When Blair tensed and quickened his movement beneath her, she was able to match him passion for passion, until, together, they reached the exquisite peak of their pleasure.

Afterward, Jan rolled over beside him and they lay in each other's arms, spent and sated.

"Jan," Blair began, but she laid a slim finger across his lips to silence him. She didn't want to hear him say that she was being overly competitive or that, good though it was, he felt less than a man for letting her make love to him. Because maybe part of what he said would be correct. She came to his apartment, but she couldn't let him have full control. Maybe being the aggressor was her way of letting him know that she wasn't giving in to him completely.

"Don't say anything," she begged. "Not now."

He kissed her fingers and nodded his agreement. They stayed that way, silent, wrapped in each other's arms, until the clock in the hallway chimed twelve times and Jan roused Blair to tell him that she wanted to go home.

"Stay," he begged. "I'll take you back to your place early in the morning.

But Jan was adamant in her desire to return to her own apartment. "What will my neighbors think," Jan asked, "if they hear me coming home early in the morning? Are you trying to ruin my spotless reputation?"

Blair laughed and reached for her, pulling her roughly into his arms and rolling across the bed, almost falling to the floor on the other side.

"You're not only beautiful," he told her, "you're also sexy and smart and funny. Why didn't some guy snatch you up a long time ago?"

"I told you why. The right guy never came along. When I was a little girl I already had a picture of the man I wanted to marry tucked away in a corner of my mind."

"Oh? And what's so unique about your very own Prince Charming?" Blair asked.

"A lot of things." Her hand lifted the thick sandy hair that had tumbled across his broad forehead. "His sandy hair, which has a habit of falling into his eyes, his clear green eyes, which seem to be different every time I look into them. Those are the physical things, but there's a lot more to him than that."

Blair shook his head and a look of concern crossed his face, and Jan thought of the sun hiding behind a cloud, turning the sky suddenly dark.

"What is it?" she asked, sensitive to his changed mood.

"I wonder if you're real, if any of this is real. I'm afraid I'm going to wake up and find it gone."

She saw that he was serious and it touched her more than anything else he had said or done. And she could understand how he felt. When they were together, the world had the quality of a dream, a perfect fantasy. But she knew that they would wake from the dream. That was what frightened her.

Blair walked her the few blocks back to her own apartment, over her protests that she was perfectly capable of seeing herself home. He went up in the elevator with her, and at her door, he turned her into his arms.

"I hate this, Jan. I want us to be together all the time, not sneaking around as if we're ashamed that we love each other." They leaned together and Blair entwined his fingers in Jan's long hair, pulling her head back so that she would be forced to look into his eyes. "Marry me, Jan. Say 'yes' tonight and we'll get the blood tests tomorrow."

Jan silently turned out of his arms and unlocked the door to her apartment. They stepped inside and she turned to face him again.

"Don't rush me, Blair. I love you, but we're worlds apart on everything that's important to us."

"You're exaggerating again. We both want to practice law, we both want to open our own offices, we both want to marry and raise a family."

"Yes, but I want to protect the innocent—corny as that may sound to you—and you have no qualms about working for anyone at all, innocent or guilty."

That remark brought a frown of impatience to Blair's face, but Jan ignored it and rushed on. "You want to get married right away and I'm sure it wouldn't be long before you wanted to have children. You want a wife, not a law partner. But I want to establish my career before I commit myself to you or anyone else."

"I think you're trying to say that your idealism would clash with my realism," Blair said, a smile crinkling the corners of his green eyes.

"Well, that's one way of putting it," Jan answered as she walked into the kitchen and busied herself with the coffeepot.

"Did I ever tell you that I used to be an idealist, too? Don't laugh, it's true. I started law school with my full share of youthful zeal and enthusiasm. I thought I could change the world. But it didn't take me long to find out that I was dreaming."

"And I'm *still* dreaming, is that what you're trying to say?"

"You're a very smart woman, Jan, and I think you have a profitable career in front of you, if—"

"If?" Jan prompted.

"If you just learn how to live in the real world," Blair finished. "Go to work, do your job, bring home your paycheck. Do your best, but don't let it drain your blood. Don't build your job up to be the most important thing in your life."

"Is that what you think I'm doing?"

"Well, isn't it?" He was leaning against the doorway between the living room and the kitchen. His broad shoulders nearly filled the door and Jan saw him suddenly as a threat, a barrier between her and the rest of the world. "Take this damned Downing case. You're letting that woman's problems take precedence over your own. If it wasn't for Carole Downing, you and I might get someplace."

"You really dislike Carole, don't you?"

"I don't like her or dislike her; I just don't like the way she's getting to you."

"Oh, I know how you feel about the Downing case," Jan said, hands on her slim hips, head tilted at an angle, dark blue eyes flashing danger signals.

"You don't have any idea how I feel, Jan, because you never take time to listen."

"All right, I'm listening." But she still held the

same pose and the same light continued to flash in her blue eyes.

"Okay," Blair answered carefully. "You think I want to marry you and chain you in the kitchen, get you pregnant right away and then insist that you stay home and be a good mommy. But you haven't gotten that from me—that's something you cooked up in your feverish little mind. I know how important your career is to you, and that's fine with me. It's great. I don't mind being married to a lawyer. What worries me is that sometimes you forget you're human. You behave like a damned legal machine, digesting facts and spewing out justice."

"And what about you? Are you any better? My God, you'd represent Jack the Ripper if there was money in it."

"You damned well bet I would. But not for the money, you're wrong about that. I'd do it because it's my job. I'm not a judge, I'm a lawyer, and a damned good one."

"Well, I'm damned good, too," Jan answered. She turned her back to him and fussed with the coffeepot, to hide the hot tears that were welling up in her eyes and running down her face.

"Why do we always have to be in competition, Jan? You're so afraid to let me get ahead of you. Even in the bedroom, you seem to feel you have to prove your superiority. Like tonight . . ."

Jan could feel a blush spreading across her cheeks and she looked down at the counter for several long moments before turning and raising her eyes to Blair's.

"I thought that you—" Embarrassment forced her to look away from the arrogant grin that was spreading on his handsome face.

"That I liked it? Are you kidding? I wasn't complaining, sweetheart. Just making a point."

"I think I missed the point," Jan answered, her embarrassment turning to anger. "Unless the point was that you'd rather I stayed in my place and stopped cramping your style."

"You're not cramping my style, Jan," Blair answered easily, "but your competitive attitude is damaging our relationship."

"I hate that holier-than-thou attitude, Blair. If you're so damned afraid that I'll get the better of you, either in court or in the bedroom, then maybe we'd just better admit that this relationship isn't going anyplace."

"Hey, this started out as a friendly discussion," Blair said, color rising in his cheeks. "I can't believe that we're standing here screaming at each other at one o'clock in the morning."

"You're right," Jan answered coldly. She marched past Blair and through the living room to the front door, which she flung open and held wide for his exit.

"Jan, I'm not going to take much more of this," Blair said, his voice as cold as hers. "Either we settle this tonight or we forget it. I'm serious. I'm tired of trying to anticipate your moods."

"I was never moody before I met you," Jan answered.

"Close the door and talk to me, Jan."

When Jan continued to hold the door open, Blair stormed out of the apartment without so much as a glance at her icy profile. He would have seen, had he looked, that her grimace was composed of a combination of anger and pain.

After she closed the door, her control finally snapped and rivers of tears streamed down her cheeks. She wrapped her arms around herself and swayed back and forth in the empty apartment, racked with spasms of heart-deep pain and sorrow. Now she had done exactly what she had sworn she would *never* do. She had lost Blair. She wasn't even sure how the argument had started or what had caused them to both become so angry. Well, maybe it's better this way, she tried to tell herself. Now you can concentrate all of your energy where it belongs, on your career and your future. But what kind of future would she have without Blair?

Chapter Twelve

Jan had little time to lament the disintegration of her personal life. The Downing trial was only a week away and there was still a lot of work to be done on the case. She knew that this was one case she didn't dare lose, not after what she had sacrificed for it. Not if she wanted to be able to hold her head up and face Blair Wynter again.

Several times during the next few days she wiped tears from her eyes. She also tried, unsuccessfully, to as easily wipe away the traces of Blair Wynter from her life.

But that was harder to do. In her weaker moments, Jan would wonder about the rest of her life, about what it would be like through all the coming years without Blair. His physical absence from her life was an almost unendurable pain and she knew that leaving New York and putting distance between them would make little difference. She would never be able to forget him, no matter how far she went. His eyes, his smile, the way he could awaken smoldering fires of passion with a look or a touch.

But drawing on the deep reserves of her inner strength, Jan survived, and outwardly, she did it admirably.

She refused to delegate any of the legal research

for the cases she was handling to the firm's law clerks, not questioning their competency, but needing the extra work to fill up all the long hours. After days spent running back and forth between the courthouse, her office, and the law library, she fell into bed exhausted. Usually, before she had cracked the files she'd carried home from the office, she was asleep. If anyone at the office noticed how hard she was pushing they chose not to mention it. Once or twice she noticed that Mark was watching her with a rather melancholy look on his face, but she made it clear that she didn't want to discuss her personal life, and Mark respected her wishes.

Every time the telephone rang, she wanted it to be Blair. Some part of her begged and prayed for it to be him. But if it had been, she probably wouldn't have talked to him. She would just have known that he was there, on the other end of the telephone line, waiting to hear her voice. That would have been enough. But he didn't call and there was no reason why he should. All of the pretrial work was finished and there was no logical reason why the Downing case couldn't be tried on schedule. There was just no reason for him to call, she had made that clear to him. But that didn't make it hurt any less when he didn't.

On the first day of the trial, Jan awakened early with an upset stomach and a pounding headache. Her awareness that the condition was caused by nerves didn't make it any easier to deal with. Somehow, she managed to keep down a cup of mild tea, to dress conservatively in a navy wool suit, and to make it to the courthouse on time.

Blair was already there, deep in conversation with his client at the plaintiff's table. Jan's heart almost stood still when she saw him, face turned away from her, sandy head inclined toward John Downing. She wanted so badly for him to turn toward her, to favor her with his lazy, insolent grin, to make everything right, just the way it used to be. But Blair didn't look up and Jan tiptoed back into the hallway to wait for her client.

Carole arrived in the next elevator and Jan led her to the defense table, studiously avoiding as much as a glance in Blair's direction.

Custody cases were usually conducted at the judge's discretion as to formality, without necessarily following the rigid rules set down for other trials. Since Judge Sara Miller was presiding, it would be simply a matter of the petitioner stating his reasons for filing the petition for custody, the respondent stating her side of the case, and both parties calling their witnesses and introducing their evidence, if any. Judge Miller was a very respected jurist with a reputation for being fair, and Jan was glad that the Downing case had been assigned to her.

Since John was the petitioner, Blair presented his case first. Although Jan tried to keep her mind on his arguments, she could not help but notice how terribly handsome he looked, and she was pleased that the case wasn't being heard before a jury. Surely the female members of the jury would have been swayed by the sight of Blair in a tan three-piece suit that fit him like a glove, with his mop of unruly hair and his compelling pale-green eyes.

Yes, if there were a jury present, Jan would probably be ready to concede defeat before Blair had even opened his mouth to present his client's position.

When he did speak, a shock of recognition reverberated through Jan's slim body. It seemed too long since she had heard his voice, could it possibly have been just a week since the argument in her apartment? The deep, resonant tones of his speech wafted around her, and for several minutes she forgot to pay strict attention to what he was saying. But then, thankfully, Jan's instinct for self-preservation took over and snapped her out of her romantic reverie.

She began to listen intently, not to Blair's voice but to his words, jotting notes on the yellow legal pad in front of her.

After Blair had laid the background of the couple's marriage, separation, and subsequent divorce, he got right to the petition for custody of the children.

"John Downing has remarried, your Honor," Blair said, "and both he and his wife are upstanding citizens of the community. They—"

"Objection, your Honor." Jan was on her feet almost before the words were out of Blair's mouth. "Mr. Wynter is unfairly implying that my client is *not* an upstanding citizen."

Blair remained facing the judge, his back stiff and unyielding.

"Objection overruled. I took no such implication from Mr. Wynter's statement."

Without so much as a glance in Jan's direction, Blair went on to present his client's case. With John's help, Blair painted a rosy picture of John and Lisa's marriage, trying to convince the judge what a wonderful home they could provide for the children. Blair managed to bring out the fact that Carole worked long hours at her business and didn't spend enough time with the children. He tried his best to make all of the trouble between the Downings, as well as their divorce, seem to be Carole's fault.

At points in John's testimony, the judge seemed

to be quite impressed, and Jan noticed that Carole didn't look quite as confident as she had before John started talking. Just wait, Jan said silently, it will be our turn next.

Finally, Judge Miller tired of John's rather repetitious monologue and politely cut it short.

Blair stepped back and turned John Downing over to Jan.

"I have no questions at this time, your Honor, but I would like to question Mr. Downing at a later time, if that pleases the court."

The judge looked rather surprised, but granted Jan's request. With Carole on the stand, Jan introduced affidavits from several people praising her devotion and dedication to her children. With careful questioning, Jan was able to contradict Blair's statements about Carole's long hours and her alleged neglect of the children's welfare. She brought out the fact that Missy's mysterious illnesses at the time of the divorce had been rooted in psychological problems caused by her father's desertion. Carole was an excellent witness and things worked pretty well for them until Blair stood up to question Carole.

"Mrs. Downing," Blair asked, "have you ever had a problem with alcohol or drugs?"

Well, Jan thought, you had to give him credit for getting right to the point. Carole glanced in Jan's direction for guidance, and Jan nodded imperceptibly, encouraging Carole to answer the question truthfully.

"I usually have a drink or two after dinner," Carole answered.

"A drink or two?" Blair asked as his eyebrows shot up in the gesture that was heartbreakingly familiar to Jan. "Is that all?"

"Sometimes it's more than that," Carole admitted.

"How much more?" he asked easily.

"I don't know exactly. I don't keep track."

"You don't keep track," Blair repeated. "Does that mean that you don't actually *know* how much you drink, Mrs. Downing?"

"No, I—" Carole was becoming flustered, but she regained control of herself quickly. "Saying that I don't keep track simply means that I don't count my after-dinner drinks."

"Fair enough. How much liquor would you say you consume weekly?"

"Again, I'm not sure. A bottle of wine, I guess."

"A bottle? Come on, Mrs. Downing, that could mean anything from a split to a gallon jug. Could you be a little more specific?"

"Objection," Jan interjected loudly as she jumped to her feet. "Your Honor, counsel is badgering the witness."

"Sustained. Be a little more careful, Mr. Wynter," the judge cautioned.

"Yes, your Honor. All right, Mrs. Downing, let's assume that you buy a couple of gallons of wine each week. Do you have many guests in the course of a week's time?"

"No, not many. One or two perhaps."

"And are these one or two weekly guests heavy drinkers?"

"*None* of my friends are heavy drinkers," Carole answered, her anger beginning to come through in the tone of her voice.

"Then I assume that you yourself are drinking most of whatever you purchase?"

Jan had one hand positioned on the edge of the table, ready to pull herself to her feet for another objection. She knew where Blair's questions were leading, and even though she had every intention of allowing Carole to admit to her drinking problem, she could not help but be irritated by the way Blair was approaching it. But she had to grant him one thing—he had a courtroom manner that made him a formidable opponent.

"I don't feel obligated to finish off everything in the house before I go out and buy another bottle," Carole answered, bringing a smile to Jan's lips.

Blair walked casually back to his table, avoiding Jan's questioning gaze. He picked up a small white piece of paper, then walked slowly back to stand in front of Carole Downing. Jan recognized his lack of haste as another tactic, designed to build up tension in the witness, as she wondered what he was getting ready to spring on her.

He stood just a few feet from Carole now, rocking back and forth on his heels.

"Mrs. Downing, I have here a copy of your monthly account with Parkway Liquors. I don't want to have to embarrass you by reading the figures on this statement aloud. So that I don't have to do that, would you like to agree with me that you buy and, by your own admission, consume one hell of a lot of liquor?"

Carole's face had gone the color of dirty snow. Her lips were trembling and tears were dropping down her cheeks. She had been well prepared by Jan and she had known this would happen, but that foreknowledge wasn't making it any easier to face Blair's demeaning questions.

"Would you like a short recess so that you can compose yourself, Mrs. Downing?" the judge asked solicitously.

"No, thank you, your Honor," Carole answered quietly. "In answer to your last question, yes, I guess I do consume too much liquor. At least, I did.

If you went to search my house today, you wouldn't find a drop."

"Oh, really?" Blair didn't quite succeed in keeping the sarcasm out of his voice. "And why is that?"

"Because my analyst has convinced me that drinking is self-destructive."

Jan was pleased to note that Blair's surprised expression was mirrored on John Downing's face as he stared at his ex-wife in openmouthed amazement.

"Are you trying to tell me that you no longer drink, Mrs. Downing?" Blair asked incredulously.

"That's correct," Carole answered evenly.

"In that case, I commend you for your courage," Blair said. "I have no further questions at this time."

Jan stood and walked to the witness stand. Although there were still tears in her eyes, Carole was able to return Jan's smile.

Blair and John Downing were deep in whispered conversation, but Jan was aware that Blair's head shot up as she walked past his table. She felt as though his eyes were boring into her back, and she longed to turn and look into his clear green eyes. Slightly disconcerted, she began to talk to Carole.

"Carole, would you like to tell us a little about your analyst and what he's doing to help you?" she asked.

"His name is Arthur Green. He's a certified psychologist who's been working with alcoholics for the past twenty years. I imagine what I'm getting from him is very similar to the Alcoholics Anonymous material. He probably doesn't have a very unique approach to my problem. All I know is that I trust him and he's helping me understand why I drank and how self-destructive my drinking was."

"Do you have any alcohol in either your home or your office at this time?"

"No, none."

"What did you do with the liquor you had at home, Carole?" Jan asked. "How did you get rid of it?"

"I poured it down the drain," Carole answered with a deep sigh.

"Was that hard for you to do?"

"Yes, it was terribly hard."

"Do you think you'll ever take another drink?"

"I don't know," Carole answered truthfully. "But I hope I don't."

"Thank you, Carole. I have no further questions, your Honor."

"Mr. Wynter?" The judge turned to Blair.

"Just one more question, Mrs. Downing." Blair stood and walked up to Carole, passing Jan as she returned to her table. She caught a whiff of his after-shave and his jacket brushed her arm as they passed, and she was glad that she could sit down and regain her composure before she had to speak again. She felt as though all the air had been forcibly drawn out of her lungs, almost as though someone had struck her a physical blow.

"How many times have you seen your Mr. Arthur Green?" Blair asked.

"Six or seven times, I believe," Carole answered.

"Over what length of time?"

"I've been seeing him less than a month," Carole answered reluctantly. It was a question they had hoped Blair wouldn't think to ask. Blair sat down and Jan knew that he had just scored a point. Surely the judge wasn't naïve enough to believe that it was coincidence that Carole had stopped drinking just a few weeks before the trial.

Well, I can't expect him to make it easy for me, Jan thought. But would I have expected it if we were still lovers? Yes, I might have, she admitted to herself, but I would have been wrong. She had a sudden insight that, although she had been the one who kept insisting that she and Blair keep their professional and private lives separate, she had also been the one who would have wanted personal favors from Blair when their professional lives meshed. Was that what he meant when he told me that I expected too much from my colleagues? she wondered. Jan's musings were interrupted by the rap of the judge's gavel, announcing that there would be a two-hour break for lunch.

Blair and John hurried out of the courtroom ahead of Jan and Carole. Carole was suffering from a bad headache, so Jan took her back to the office and let her rest in the conference room while she answered some of her phone calls. Then they grabbed a quick sandwich at a deli on their way back to the courthouse.

As soon as court reconvened, John Downing took the stand again.

"Mr. Downing," Jan asked, "what kind of a relationship do you have with your father?"

"Objection, your Honor!" Although Jan had expected Blair to object, she hadn't expected him to do it quite that soon.

"Overruled, Mr. Wynter. We'll give Ms. Richmond a chance to tie this in."

"Thank you, your Honor," Jan answered, aware of Blair's anger filling the room behind her. "Please answer the question, Mr. Downing."

"My father and I have a good relationship," John answered cautiously, obviously not trusting her.

Jan nodded and continued, knowing that Carole was holding her breath at the defense table.

"Your father was an alcoholic, wasn't he?" Jan asked. John Downing's reaction was exactly what she and Carole had expected. His eyes shot to the defense table with a look that bored into the top of Carole's bowed head. He was silently accusing her of breaking a family confidence, as she had known he would. Carole had very reluctantly told Jan about John's father's problem, and she had strongly objected to Jan's using it.

"Your Honor, I must again object to this line of questioning," Blair shouted.

"Ms. Richmond, can you show me that this line of questioning has any relevance to the custody case we're hearing today?" Judge Miller asked.

"I think it has a great deal of relevance, your Honor," Jan answered. "I believe Mr. Downing's testimony will show that he has some personal experience with drinking problems and that—"

"That has absolutely nothing to do with the question of custody in this case, your Honor." Blair's face was livid with anger and the eyes that he finally turned on Jan were narrowed menacingly.

"I disagree, Mr. Wynter," Jan shot back before the judge had a chance to rule on the objection. "That's what this entire hearing is about, and if I can prove that John Downing—"

"Ms. Richmond, let's not turn this hearing into a shouting match," the judge said, raising her voice. "I'm afraid I have to agree with Mr. Wynter. Objection sustained."

Jan accepted the judge's ruling and dismissed John Downing. She was sorry that Blair hadn't waited a few minutes longer to voice his objection. But maybe she had gotten enough into the record

and into the judge's consciousness. She had had
barely enough time to plant the idea in the judge's
mind that John's father had been an alcoholic and
that John thought they had a good relationship.
Now she could only hope that the judge would make
the necessary connections: John was bringing up
Carole's drinking problem because he had a deep-
seated fear of alcoholism, caused by his father's
problem. John loved his father and insisted that
they had a good relationship, ergo a good relationship was possible between Carole, who also was a
reformed drinker, and her children.

It was certainly a weak point at best, and maybe
it wouldn't do their case any good. But it was worth
a try. Of course, Jan had hoped to get in the facts
that John's father had stopped drinking and become a model father to his children, that he was
still living today, that he and John were still very
close, and that John hadn't been harmed, either
physically or psychologically, by his father's fight
against alcoholism.

Jan walked back to the defense table on shaky
legs and sat down gratefully. She wasn't sure if she
was shaking from her interrogation of John Downing or from her contact with Blair. Fighting Blair
in the courtroom was exactly what she had expected it to be, exactly what she had feared. Every
word he spoke was weighed and taken on a personal level, every gesture he made was examined
minutely. Jan had not too long ago been sure of
beating him in court. Now she wondered how she
could have ever been so stupid. No matter how
well-qualified she was, she wouldn't have a chance
against him, because she was letting her personal
feelings for him get in the way of her professionalism.
She had never before trembled walking back and

forth to the witness stand, or raised her voice to opposing counsel. Or wanted to reach out and touch him. She was performing badly, and she knew it. She could only hope that it wasn't as obvious to the judge as it was to her.

She reached over and squeezed Carole's cold hands reassuringly as she examined Judge Miller's face for a clue as to her feeling about the case. But the judge's face was stoic. Her eyes gave nothing away as they passed over the attorneys and their clients. She assured all parties that her decision would be made within seventy-two hours, then stood and left the courtroom.

Jan pulled herself to her feet and glanced covertly in Blair's direction. He was shoving file folders and legal pads into his briefcase with hurried movements. As soon as the judge was out of the room, he patted John's shoulder and walked rapidly down the aisle, his eyes fixed on something in the distance. Jan's heart turned over as she realized that all along she had hoped that the trial would bring them back together. But it was all too clear that she had lost him for good. She forced herself to smile at Carole and offer some words of encouragement.

"How do you think it went?" Carole asked, anxious for reassurance.

"It's hard to say," Jan answered, "but we made some points."

"Do you think she'll decide in our favor?" Carole pressed.

"I make it a point never to anticipate a judge's decision," Jan answered. But when she saw the crestfallen look on Carole's face, she knew that she couldn't leave the woman in such misery. "I think we did it, Carole. But remember, I'm not the judge.

And Sara Miller is only human, a lawyer who has been elevated to a judgeship for very human considerations. She's a fair woman. If she can find her way clear to let you keep the children without compromising her standards, she will."

"I don't know how to ever thank you for all you've done, Jan," Carole said, close to tears again.

"You already have thanked me," Jan answered warmly.

They went down in the elevator together, and when she parted with Carole on the courthouse steps, Jan felt suddenly alone and lonely. For a week she had looked forward to the trial, knowing that she would see Blair there. She had hoped, without ever voicing the hope, that he would look at her or speak to her, letting her know that he still cared. Now the trial was over, and that hope had been dashed by the harsh winds of reality. She remembered how she had once thought that winning the Downing case would put her on top of the world. Now, she admitted as she walked slowly in the direction of her office, winning or losing hardly mattered.

Chapter Thirteen

∾

While Jan waited for the judge's decision to be handed down, she started to clean out her desk at Babcock, Wynne & Whitmann. Whether she won or lost the case made little difference. It was time for a change. She was sorry that Mark was out of town on a case, because she would have liked to talk to him. But maybe it would be better this way, she reasoned. Maybe she needed to make this decision on her own, without Mark's influence.

She packed boxes of law books, made notations on files that would have to be turned over to other members of the firm for completion. Barbra was in tears when she surmised that Jan was leaving, but her tears dried up when Jan promised to steal her away from Babcock, Wynne as soon as she was established in an office of her own. Even the prospect of a hefty cut in salary didn't dampen Barbra's enthusiasm. Jan wasn't taking the step blindly. She knew that she would probably make a lot less money on her own than she made working for Mark. She was fully aware that she might have to sacrifice her wonderful apartment and give up many of the little luxuries she now took for granted. Anyway, everything in her apartment reminded her of the time she had spent with Blair and it pained her to constantly view objects that held memories of those happier days. The wound caused by the loss of Blair was raw, reopened by seeing him on the day of the trial and, in effect, losing him all over again.

Any material sacrifices she had to make would only be for as long as it took for her to establish her own practice. And maybe they would even help to get her mind off the greater losses in her life.

Jan wasn't afraid of the future, just eager to get on with it.

On the third morning after the trial, just as she was finishing her packing, a hand-delivered packet arrived on Jan's desk. It was Judge Miller's decision. With trembling hands, Jan removed the official decree from the envelope and began to read. It took her only a moment to get the gist of the order and she suddenly felt like running out of her office, shouting to the entire office staff that she had won. The decree granted temporary custody of Missy and John to their mother, subject to a reevaluation in six month's time. Subject, Jan knew without having to see it in print, to Carole's success in winning her battle against alcoholism.

Jan's first moment of elation was quickly followed by a hollow feeling of sadness. Poor Blair, she thought, no matter how he tried to deny it, the case had to be important to him too. And I've beat him. He must be miserable.

In the following hours there was none of the great sense of triumph Jan had expected. She had emerged victorious only to find that her victory was an empty one. For one thing, she was seeing the Downing case in its proper perspective—it was not nearly as important as she had built it up to be. *Every* case a lawyer handled was important to a degree, but the Downing case was, after all, just another case. Because of the timing, she had hung all of her hopes on this one. If it had come along at any other time in her life, she might have hardly noticed it or distinguished it from the bulk of her work load.

She telephoned Carole to give her the news, and her client's happy tears reassured Jan that it had been worth her efforts, at least in one sense, and that the judge's decision was the right one. She could hear Johnny and Missy's joyous shouts in the background as their mother told them the good news and she hung up the phone feeling better. Then Barbra was at the door, telling her that Mark was back in his office waiting to talk to her. Taking a deep breath and squaring her shoulders, Jan headed down the hallway to his office. She knew that she would have to tell him of her empty success, and also tell him that she was leaving. She only hoped that he wouldn't try to convince her to stay. She had lost one dream by losing Blair Wynter. Now it was more important than ever that she pursue her other dream and make it come true.

Mark rose from his desk and came to meet her in the middle of the room, beaming from ear to ear.

"Congratulations, Janelle. I hear you did a fine job. I only wish I could have been there to see you in action."

"Thank you, Mark," Jan answered, her blue eyes suddenly wet with tears.

"What is it, Janelle?" Mark asked, alarm spreading on his handsome face. "I thought you'd be sprinkling sunshine all over the office today."

"I don't know why you gave me the Downing case, Mark. It's caused me so much misery. And I didn't even do a very good job on it."

"I gave it to you because you're a good lawyer

and a compassionate person, just the combination the case needed," Mark answered, wiping the tears from her eyes. "And you did a marvelous job on it. I just had breakfast with Sara Miller and she was very impressed. She says you tried your best to slip in some inadmissible testimony about John's father." Mark chuckled. "Even though she couldn't allow it, she seems to have admired your nerve."

"That wasn't very fair to Blair, was it?" Jan asked.

"Is that what's bothering you? Believe me, Jan, Blair Wynter would have done the same thing to you, given the chance. He's one hell of a good lawyer and he wouldn't have given you an inch. Stu Underwood's going to hate to lose him."

"Is he leaving Stu's firm?" Jan asked with alarm. "Where is he going?"

"Rumor has it that he's going to open his own office," Mark answered. Then, taking Jan's hand in his, he told her quietly, "I'm going to hate losing you, too, Janelle."

"Oh, Mark, who told you? I was going to tell you myself."

"I know you were, but you can't keep a secret long in an office this size. Oh, don't look like that, I'm not going to try to talk you out of it. I just want you to know that you can stay here until you get everything squared away. Stay as long as you want to stay, not a minute longer. Fair enough?"

"Too fair. You're far too good to me, Mark."

"Janelle, I don't know exactly what the problem is between you and Blair Wynter, but if it's something that you can patch up, why don't you try?"

"Oh, Mark, we disagree on so many things."

"Important things?"

"Of course they're important! He wants to get

married right away and have children. He wants to practice corporate law."

"Is there something wrong with the practice of corporate law?" Mark asked.

"No, of course not. But we're just so . . . so *different*. We don't have the same values."

"I think you do."

"But you don't understand, Mark."

"Janelle," Mark said, lifting her chin so that her eyes met his, "is there anything or anyone in your life as important as Blair Wynter?"

"No!" she answered without thinking. Then, as she understood what she had said, a smile lit up Jan's lovely face and her eyes sparkled with a new light.

"Go after him, Janelle," Mark told her, "and don't worry so much about your career and how it will suffer. The law is the first love of my life, but it is not a strict, unbendable mistress. The law can bend, it can find room for compromise, for compassion. If it couldn't, I think I would have switched my allegiance to another mistress long ago. And I'm sure Blair Wynter feels the same."

"Thank you, Mark. My father was right about you. You really are the best substitute father a girl could have."

Mark called her back as she was about to slip through the door. "Jan, when you think you're ready to break out on your own, come and talk to me first. I'd like to make a little investment in your future."

"You already have," Jan told him as she came back to his desk, leaned over, and kissed him soundly on the cheek. "You already have."

Jan went back to her office, humming a happy tune under her breath. Why had it taken Mark to make her realize that the solution to her problem was so simple? She was always talking about "priorities," so why hadn't she realized that Blair Wynter deserved top priority in her life? Her mind was now a clear landscape brushed clean by a strong wind. Now she was ready to build on a strong foundation of love. She could only hope that Blair felt the same way she did.

The next morning, Jan jumped out of bed before the alarm went off, donned a new powder-blue jogging suit, and went to the park to wait for Blair. She took a position beside the track, about halfway around the lake, and had no intention of moving until Blair showed up. She hadn't decided what she would do if this turned out to be the one day of the year he decided not to run. She also didn't have any idea what she was going to say to him. She would cross that bridge when she came to it.

The minutes dragged by like hours until Blair finally appeared around the bend of the track, wearing the old gray jogging suit he practically lived in. When he spotted Jan obviously waiting for him, he visibly slowed his pace, and for a long moment she was afraid that he would change direction to avoid a confrontation.

When he picked up his pace again and continued to move toward her, Jan knew that she had him.

As he approached the spot where she was waiting, Jan moved gracefully onto the track and started to run beside him. For a few moments they ran in silence. Jan cleared her throat to speak, but the words stuck in her throat. She began to think that she had made a terrible mistake, that Blair had nothing to say to her, and that her own vocal cords had frozen her into permanent silence.

Then Blair turned toward her, without a break in his easy stride.

"I guess I should offer my congratulations, Counselor," he said, the familiar grin spreading across his handsome face and warming Jan's cold body like the first rays of the summer sun.

"It was a lucky win," Jan conceded graciously, her heart doing flipflops in her chest at the sound of Blair's deep, resonant voice.

"Well, Carole Downing gets to keep her children. That's what you wanted, and you got it."

"Yes, but she's willing to let John and Lisa have them for two entire months in the summer. I think that should make everyone happy, especially Johnny and Missy."

"They're a couple of great kids, and they really love their mother," Blair admitted. "I don't feel too badly about losing this one, especially since I know that Carole's getting help with her drinking problem."

"They love their father, too, so I guess he can't be all bad. Even though I really wanted to believe that he is," Jan said truthfully.

"Both Carole and John are good people," Blair answered. "There's a little bit of good in just about everyone. But I guess nobody comes up smelling like a rose when you start to air their private lives in public."

They each turned to their own thoughts and ran in silence for another minute or so before Jan spoke again.

"Blair, I've been thinking about that last night we were together, the things we argued about. None of them were really important, were they?"

"No, they weren't."

"Even the Downing case wasn't that important.

It was just the timing, the fact that it was the last case I'd handle for Mark, before breaking out on my own. I became obsessed with winning it, and after a while I couldn't even discuss it rationally."

"I knew that," Blair admitted, "and I guess I should have been more understanding. But I let the damned case get under my skin, too. I behaved very selfishly."

"It takes a big man to admit he's been wrong, Blair," Jan said without cracking a smile.

He laughed and slowed his pace slightly as he turned toward her. "You're really something, do you know that?"

Jan wanted to come back with a quick rejoinder, but she suddenly realized that she was exhausted, both mentally and physically. The pace of the past few weeks had finally taken their toll. Besides, there was always a feeling of letdown after a long-awaited trial was finally over.

Blair was running slightly ahead of her, and for another minute or so she tried to match his stride and keep up with him. Then she started to fall behind and she panicked. She couldn't give up, because if she did she would be showing her weakness, letting him know that he was stronger than she was. Winning had always been so important to her, whether she was running or arguing a case or playing chess or—

Abruptly, Jan stopped in her tracks and waited patiently while Blair discovered her absence from his side, made a small circle in the track, and jogged back to her.

"What's wrong?" he asked solicitously.

"I'm tired. You're too fast for me," Jan admitted, waiting for the teasing remark that she knew would come.

"Are you actually admitting that you can't keep up with me?" Blair asked before he suddenly decided to change his tack. "I'm kind of tired myself. All these long weeks of grueling competition have gotten to me, too."

Jan laughed and threw herself down on the grass beside the track.

"Do you realize this is almost the exact spot where we first met?" Blair asked, bending over her and favoring her with his warmest smile.

"Yes, I know," she answered quietly. "Why do you think I picked this spot to stop running? And I mean that literally, Blair. I have really stopped running."

"In spite of your liberated ways, you're really quite a romantic lady," Blair commented, dropping down on the grass beside her with the easy fluidity of movement that had first so intrigued her.

"Blair," she began, "I have something to ask you. Do you think we could—"

"Stop! Not another word." Blair laid a gentle finger across Jan's mouth, then touched the spot with his lips.

It was now Jan's turn to raise her brows, her blue eyes asking an unspoken question.

"I have a feeling that I know what you were going to ask," Blair explained, his green eyes sparkling with mischief. "And I absolutely refuse to let *you* propose to *me*."

"But I wasn't—"

"It's about time we stopped competing and got on the same side," he went on, ignoring her protests. "How do you like the sound of Wynter and Wynter, Attorneys at Law?"

"I like it very much. I'd even agree to help you out with your big-deal corporate cases, but—"

"Just say you'll marry me, Jan. Give me a plain old-fashioned 'yes,' and I promise you you'll never be sorry. I'll baby-sit the kids, I'll help with the housework, I'll even cook dinner when you're tied up in court."

"Yes," she answered simply, gladly, to this big, strong, impossibly wonderful man whom she loved with all her heart.

"Great!" he shouted, throwing both arms straight up in the air in a gesture of victory before throwing them around Jan and roughly pulling her to him. He hugged her fiercely and kissed her eyes, her ears, her forehead, and the tip of her cold nose before he reached her waiting lips with his.

"Now"—he grinned when he finally released her—"was there something you wanted to ask me?"

"Yes, there was. I was going to ask you if we could get off this freezing grass and go find some breakfast. I'm starving!"

Blair threw back his head and laughed uproariously before taking Jan into his arms again to seal their bargain. When he had kissed her soundly and repeated his promise of lasting love, they jogged gently out of the park and into their future together.

TELL US YOUR OPINIONS AND RECEIVE A FREE COPY
OF THE RAPTURE NEWSLETTER.

Thank you for filling out our questionnaire. Your response to the following questions will help us to bring you more and better books. In appreciation of your help we will send you a free copy of the Rapture Newsletter.

1. Book Title:_____

   Book #:_____ (5-7)

2. Using the scale below how would you rate this book on the following features? Please write in one rating from 0-10 for each feature in the spaces provided. Ignore bracketed numbers.

(Poor) 0 1 2 3 4 5 6 7 8 9 10 (Excellent)
                                              0-10 Rating

Overall Opinion of Book................. _____ (8)
Plot/Story............................ _____ (9)
Setting/Location...................... _____ (10)
Writing Style......................... _____ (11)
Dialogue.............................. _____ (12)
Love Scenes........................... _____ (13)
Character Development:
Heroine:.............................. _____ (14)
Hero:................................. _____ (15)
Romantic Scene on Front Cover......... _____ (16)
Back Cover Story Outline.............. _____ (17)
First Page Excerpts................... _____ (18)

3. What is your: Education: Age:_____(20-22)

   High School ( )1   4 Yrs. College ( )3
   2 Yrs. College ( )2   Post Grad   ( )4 (23)

4. Print Name:_____

   Address:_____

   City:_____State:_____Zip:_____

   Phone # (   )_____(25)

Thank you for your time and effort. Please send to New American Library, Rapture Romance Research Department, 1633 Broadway, New York, NY 10019.

RAPTURE ROMANCE

*Provocative and sensual,
passionate and tender—
the magic and mystery of love
in all its many guises*

Coming next month

A DISTANT LIGHT by Ellie Winslow. As suddenly as he'd once disappeared, Louis Dupierre reentered Tara's life. Was it the promise of ecstasy, or some unknown, darker reason that brought him back? Tara didn't know, nor was she sure whether she could risk loving—and trusting— Louis again . . .

PASSIONATE ENTERPRISE by Charlotte Wisely. Gwen Franklin's business sense surrendered to sensual pleasure in the arms of executive Kurt Jensen. But could Gwen keep working to prove she could rise as high as any man in the corporate world—when she was falling so deeply in love?

TORRENT OF LOVE by Marianna Essex. By day, architect Erin Kelly struggled against arrogant builder Alex Butler, but at night, their lovemaking was sheer ecstasy. Yet when their project ended, so did their affair, and Erin was struggling again—to make Alex see beyond business, into her heart . . .

LOVE'S JOURNEY HOME by Bree Thomas. Soap opera star Katherine Ransom was back home—and back in the arms of Joe Mercer, the man who'd once stolen her heart. But caught up in irresistible passion, Katherine soon found herself forced to choose between her glamorous career— and Joe . . .

AMBER DREAMS by Diana Morgan. Jenny Moffatt was determined to overcome Ryan Powers and his big money interests. But instead, his incredible attractiveness awed her, and she was swept away by desire . . .

WINTER FLAME by Deborah Benét. Darcy had vowed never to see Chason again. But now her ex-husband was back, conquering her with loving caresses. If Chason wanted to reestablish their marriage, would his love be enough to help her overcome the past. . . ?

RAPTURE ROMANCE

**Provocative and sensual,
passionate and tender—
the magic and mystery of love
in all its many guises**

NEW Titles Available Now

*Price is $2.25 in Canada

To order, use coupon on next page

RAPTURE ROMANCE

Provocative and sensual, passionate and tender— the magic and mystery of love in all its many guises

Buy them at your local

bookstore or use coupon

on next page for ordering.

RAPTURE ROMANCE

*Provocative and sensual,
passionate and tender—
the magic and mystery of love
in all its many guises*

SPECIAL $1.00 REBATE OFFER
WHEN YOU BUY
FOUR RAPTURE ROMANCES

To receive your cash refund, send:

1. This coupon: To qualify for the $1.00 refund, this coupon, completed with your name and address, must be used. (Certificate may not be reproduced)

2. Proof of purchase: Print, on the reverse side of this coupon, the *title* of the books, the *numbers* of the books (on the upper right hand of the front cover preceding the price), and the U.P.C. numbers (on the back covers) on your next four purchases.

3. Cash register receipts, with prices circled to:
   Rapture Romance $1.00 Refund Offer
   P.O. Box NB037
   El Paso, Texas 79977

Offer good only in the U.S. and Canada. Limit one refund/response per household for any group of four Rapture Romance titles. Void where prohibited, taxed or restricted. Allow 6–8 weeks for delivery. Offer expires March 31, 1984.

NAME_____

ADDRESS_____

CITY_____STATE_____ZIP_____

SPECIAL $1.00 REBATE OFFER
WHEN YOU BUY
FOUR RAPTURE ROMANCES

See complete details on reverse

1. Book Title _____

   Book Number 451-_____

   U.P.C. Number 7116200195-_____

2. Book Title _____

   Book Number 451-_____

   U.P.C. Number 7116200195-_____

3. Book Title _____

   Book Number 451-_____

   U.P.C. Number 7116200195-_____

4. Book Title _____

   Book Number 451-_____

   U.P.C. Number 7116200195-_____

U.P.C. Number

0 SAMPLE

7 11162 00195